RISE OF MAGIC

RISE OF MAGIC

THE LEIRA CHRONICLES™ BOOK 10

MARTHA CARR

MICHAEL ANDERLE

LMBPN

DISRUPTIVE IMAGINATION

From Martha

To everyone who still believes in magic and all the possibilities that holds.

To all the readers who make this entire ride so much fun.

To Louie, Jackie, and so many wonderful friends who remind me all the time of what really matters and how wonderful life can be in any given moment.

And finally, a special thank you to John Nelson of the Austin, Texas Police Department who patiently answers all of my questions. I hope I made you proud. Thank you for your service.

From Michael

*To Family, Friends and
Those Who Love
To Read.
May We All Enjoy Grace
To Live The Life We Are
Called.*

CHAPTER ONE

Leira sat on the back porch in the dark, sipping a cold long neck. The night was quiet except for the sound of cicadas and crickets blending together and the occasional rat rummaging through the trash cans a few doors down.

She glanced up at the dim light in the Moss' bedroom window and wondered if Angel was waiting up for Matt to finish running in shifter form. "You never know what's going on behind closed doors."

Correk pushed open the screen door. "What are you doing out here? It's almost midnight."

"Enjoying the break in the action. I figure there's not going to be a lot of them. I'm going to take each one when I find them and relish them." She leaned down and picked up the beer sitting on the floor. "I saved one for you, just in case."

"I'll choose to believe that was for me," he said, taking the bottle. He sat down next to her and balanced a boot on the rail of the porch. "Have you heard from Lily?"

"I got the agreed signal from her at about six o'clock when she was on her way home. She's fine so far. Lois, on the other hand, is not too happy with us."

Correk cleared his throat and took a long swig, resting the bottle in his lap. "We've put too much on one young witch."

"Lily chose to stay at Fleeker. We need to honor that and stand next to her." Leira's phone buzzed and she took it off the banister where it was sitting. "Blocked number. Hello General." She waved at Correk as he kissed the top of her head and went inside.

"How did you know? Was that a magic thing?"

"No, I just had a feeling." Leira checked her watch. "Another late night call. We have to stop meeting like this."

"Trouble seems to like the late night hours. I have another job for you if you've got the time. It's an odd one, even for you."

"Now you're just flirting with me."

The general chuckled and let out a sigh. "I've missed talking to you, Leira. You manage to keep a sense of humor in the middle of mayhem."

"The swearing helps too."

The general laughed. "Both may be needed for this job. There's an old abandoned cruise ship off the coast of Tuscany in a place called Isola del Giglio. It hit the rocks, and no one has wanted to spend the money to break it up and haul it away. The ship has been rusting there for a good ten years and had become a home to lobsters and crabs, till about three months ago."

"What happened three months ago?"

"A new kind of underwater creature took over the ship

with a sidekick and they are using it as their home base. Are you familiar with the legend of Atlantis?"

"I've met at least one magical from Atlantis. But she walked around topside."

"Yes, well there's far more than one magical under the sea. Mermaids, Draksa. They're some kind of underwater dragons, if you can believe that. Vermillions look like Elves till you get to their face and then there's gills and a fin on top of their head. There's a reason for this zoology lesson. A Vermillion has taken over the ship and has a bonded Draksa. Can be a pretty aggressive creature. Use extreme caution. The pair is using the ship as a staging area to raid the nearby city and scare the inhabitants."

"Why are you getting involved in another country's problems?"

"It can't always work like that anymore. Magic coming back connects all of us and we're learning how to work together. Italy doesn't have someone like you and if it gets out that the ocean is full of magical creatures that don't always play nice it'll be Jaws all over again. Everybody with a boat will head out to take care of the problem."

"Plenty of people will get hurt."

Correk came back out with two more bottles and handed one to Leira, sitting down on the banister. He leaned back to get a better view of the alley and noticed the shifter in the shadows at the other end. He nodded in that direction. "Matt's trying to come home," he whispered.

Leira glanced up toward the Moss house and saw Angel step back from the window. "What exactly do you need me to do? Are you asking me to arrest these goons?" asked

Leira, getting up and taking Correk's hand. Correk opened the screen door and held it for Leira.

"I'm asking you to bring them in to face justice," said the general.

"That's different. It brings up a lot of questions. How are you going to bring magicals to court? Isn't that the Silver Griffins territory? Fuck, what kind of black site are we talking here?"

Correk arched an eyebrow and stopped where he was, suddenly listening more intently to Leira's side of the conversation.

The general sucked in air through his teeth. "We have a deal with the Silver Griffins to turn over bounties to them to send to Trevilsom Prison. We're going to do our best not to repeat the mistakes of the past. Look, I'll address the elephant in the room. No experiments just because we have them and they're not human. You have my word."

"Yeah, but do I have the word of every other government official?"

"You can be there when Lois and her crew take them. They will be nearby for backup if you need them, but I'm guessing you won't."

"That's a lot of confidence in one magical against a crew."

"I didn't say that. You'll see. I'm sending you the coordinates. You leave immediately before they raid the coastline again and someone finally gets some good footage of them that we can't explain."

The general hung up abruptly and the coordinates just as quickly appeared on her phone. Leira frowned looking at them.

"What was that all about?" asked Correk, crossing his arms over his chest.

"The general has another job for me. But this time it's gonna be a slip 'n slide with some creatures from under the sea."

They both looked up at the sound of talking from the alley, standing still as they listened to the distant hushed voices. Leira's forehead wrinkled, stepping closer to the screen door.

"Angel is a lot tougher than I gave her credit," whispered Leira, as she gently shut the back door. She leaned over and kissed Correk. "I've got to go."

"Hang on, take the troll with you. It sounds like his kind of assignment. For me... take him for me."

Leira opened a portal to the coordinates and stepped through to a small boat tied behind the large rocks. The old cruise ship was on the other side listing heavily to the starboard side with part of its deck below waters. Rust was appearing in all the joints.

The boat rocked gently as Leira stepped through, the sharp wind off the ocean catching her in the face. She shook off the blast of cold air as the portal closed, the sparks fizzing in the water.

"You okay in there? It's show time." Leira looked in her pocket at the troll, still curled up. He gave a big yawn and stretched a paw over his head. "This should be a fair match. Two for two unless there's a bonus evil doer in there." She scooped out the troll and set him on her shoulder, stepping onto the rocks and swiftly moving over the top, staying low.

Magic swirled into her feet, rising up through her body, the symbols lighting up on her arms. She got to the crest of the rocks and saw the Draksa above at the bow of the ship. He was balancing on the chrome balustrade just above the waterline. Its silver wings were open and shining under the moonlight, and it was stretching its long neck, snapping at large flies.

"A dragon?" muttered Leira. "That has to be the Draksa."

Yumfuck let out a low growl, sniffing the air. "The Vermillion is close by too. I can smell him."

"Why didn't I ever see a Vermillion on Oriceran?" Leira watched the Draksa roar, flapping its wings.

"Most of the ones on Oriceran are in Trevilsom. They're from this planet, from Atlantis, but there aren't many left of them. Kind of like Jasper Elves but with less of a sense of humor."

She looked over at the small troll on her shoulder. "You've really grown into a great warrior. Come on, let's go kick some scaly ass." Leira started to crawl up the rock but something wet and muscular firmly grasped her ankle. She dropped flat against the rock, a small fireball in her palm as she rolled over, her eyes glowing.

A mermaid was half out of the water, a hand still around Leira's ankle. A finger was pressed against her lips and on her wrist a tattoo was visible of two S's intertwined. Floating just behind her were three other mermaids, their long hair in braids tied with pieces of seaweed.

The mermaid gestured to Leira to follow along the rocks to the left and the back of the ship. The others bobbed under the surface, glimmers of silver or blue moving underwater toward the far side of the ship. Leira followed, picking her way across the rocks, the troll hanging onto her shoulder, bouncing up and down.

The ocean spray was making her shoes damp and the rocks slippery.

They got to the edge of the rocks, the sea lapping at the ship. A mermaid with dark hair pointed at a thick chain that hung down from the side of the boat where the anchor used to be connected, and then up at the deck tilted into the air.

Leira looked up, her eyes glowing and set an intention. *Find the Vermillion.* A thread of magic crept up the side of the ship and over the edge at the top, showing Leira the layout.

The mermaids exchanged glances, clustered together at the surface. "What is she doing?" asked the dark-haired mermaid.

The Vermillion was sitting on a hatch cover with peeling grey paint, his elbow on his knee and his chin resting in his hand. There was a tall red fin along the top of his head and webbing between his fingers. He was tossing a glowing ball of iridescent blue glob up and down in his hand, staring toward the coast. "Jameer," he shouted, "How do you feel about a night out?"

The Draksa spread its wings and lifted into the air, flapping in long, quick motions with its legs dangling beneath. It landed close to the Vermillion on the uneven deck of the flying bridge, digging its claws in just above where the Vermillion was resting.

"I could use a few new baubles." The Draksa filled its chest with air and lifted its head to roar, the sound echoing over the open water. Lights blinked on in windows along the shore.

Jameer breathed in again but stopped midway, snapping its jaws shut and looking around, the leathery wings opening and closing.

"What is it?" The Vermillion stood up and looked around but didn't see anything. Leira's energy swirled in on itself, hidden as it went around him. It brushed up against his magic, taking measure of the creature.

It was the closest Leira had ever let her magic get to an enemy without their notice and to her surprise it was working.

To a point.

The Vermillion grew agitated and stomped over to the edge of the ship, looking down. All but one of the mermaids ducked under the water in time, but one was just a second too slow, her tail flapping against the water, sending out ripples. The Vermillion's irises widened from slits into spheres, zeroing in on the water below.

"Jameer, looks like we're doing a little fishing first. There are nosey intruders. You feeling a little hungry?"

The Draksa flew down by the Vermillion's side, his claws around the balustrade, peering over the side. "Did I ever tell you I'm a pescatarian?"

"You're a damn liar," said the Vermillion, loading up a spear gun. "I saw you take down that deer last week."

"That was last week. You going old school? What's with the spear?"

"It's gotten too easy. I'm bored."

Leira pulled her energy back and looked down at the

symbols on her arms. There were a few different possible outcomes. "Not going to be as easy as I thought," she whispered to Yumfuck.

"Sounds like an adventure. Let's take down these wannabe rulers of a rusty bucket."

"Well said, like a poem." Leira gave a crooked smile as she pulled herself up the side of the ship by the heavy chain, her magic staying just ahead of her. Yumfuck held onto her shoulder like he was surfing a wave. When they got just below the top of the ship he began to grow, coming over the top at his full size and catching the Vermillion off guard.

"Aloha motherfuckers," growled the troll, a large paw swiping at the Vermillion, leaving deep claw marks in his arm and loosening his grip on the spear gun. The aquatic Elf screamed out in pain, dropping the weapon. He leapt overboard into the water far below, pointing his toes and holding his one good arm across his chest.

The Draksa flew at Yumfuck's head, its claws outstretched but Leira saw him coming and got off a fireball that hit the dragon in the chest just beneath his left shoulder. The wind was knocked out of him and he spiraled toward the water, pulling his wings in at the last moment to prevent them from breaking.

"You think that was it?" Yumfuck looked over the side.

"No, I think they took the fight below the surface." She looked up at the troll. "You stay here. You're not meant to be fighting underwater." Leira got up on the edge of the ship.

"Neither are you."

"We don't know that, and I've got a feeling the mermaids are outmatched. I'm not leaving them alone."

"If I start turning blue, I'm jumping in."

"Deal." Leira crossed her arms over her chest, the symbols spinning and dropped into the water. She sunk down four fathoms, the light from her eyes glowing in the dark waters. She looked up toward the surface and started to kick for the top to get air, but a hand yanked her sideways. Leira turned, ready to fight but found herself once again looking into the eyes of a mermaid.

The mermaid put her hands on Leira's jaw, gently forcing her to open her mouth. Leira's eyes widened but she did it as the mermaid blew bubbles across the short span. They drifted into Leira's mouth as the mermaid sung a spell that floated around Leira, wrapping her tighter and tighter.

"Can you hear me now?" asked the mermaid.

Leira nodded her head slowly.

"Stop holding your breath. You can breathe in the water for the next few hours. Go ahead, do it. We don't have much time."

A thin stream of fire shot past their heads, streaking through the water and briefly illuminating their faces. The flash startled Leira and she sucked in water, expecting to choke. She was surprised when her lungs filled and then pushed out the water again, seeking more. She gulped in more as another flash of heat sizzled in the water even closer to her head.

"Time's up!" said the mermaid, grabbing Leira by the hand and pulling her along as they swam toward the fire blasts. "You're a Jasper Elf, right?" asked the mermaid over her shoulder, her powerful wide tail moving up and down, pushing them through the water. "You can do this. Use your magic. Don't fight it or try to figure it out. That will only slow you down. Stop thinking and just go."

"You clearly don't know me." Leira shook her head, surprised that sound came out of her mouth, earning a laugh from the mermaid. The smile quickly disappeared when fire streamed over their heads, spreading out in a fan.

The mermaid ducked and pulled Leira deeper out of the direct line of fire. "Let go of what you think and go with your magic. You can do it," said the mermaid. "I've got to go help my sisters." She let go of Leira's hand and blew out a stream of bubbles, propelling herself faster through the water, her tail creating a stream behind her.

Leira could hear Turner Underwood's voice in her head. *Get out of the way and be willing to fit yourself to the energy.*

She set an intention. *Let me help.* The energy rolled around her and she started swimming, pushing through the murky waters. Finally, she saw the glint of silver ahead and realized it was the tail of a mermaid thrashing. She caught sight of the Draksa, its claws out, pulsing water toward a mermaid.

The mermaid was transformed with long talons and sharp teeth, her tail curved to her right, pushing back just as hard.

The Vermillion was holding another mermaid by the neck, leering as he moved back, fire forming in the deep waters in front of him. Nearby a mermaid floated, her head down and her hair covering her face.

Leira felt the magic lurch forward, taking hold of her and for a moment she felt the choice. The magic didn't care which way she went. She could choose to let it reach out or choose to control it. Make it fix what *she* saw as the problem.

She felt herself let go as the magic ripple out and a calm came over her. The waves of energy pounded away at everyone in its path, pushing them all apart in a widening circle, bruising their bodies. Leira outstretched her arms, fire forming in her palms. She smiled just a little as the fire shot through the water and found its first mark.

The Vermillion spun like a top, choking on the bubbles, blood droplets clinging to them. The Draksa cried out, a sharp note echoing through the water, but Leira didn't take back control. The energy washed over him, pushing him further down and the pressure built around his wings.

The last she saw of the creature was his face scarcely visible in the darkness, its mouth open in a scream and the barely audible sound of snapping bones in his wings.

Leira felt the energy returning to her, diminishing as the Vermillion's chin dropped forward and his arms floated up in the direction of the surface, the bloody bubbles following the same path.

Two of the mermaids took the arms of their fallen sister and began to swim away. Leira looked up toward the surface and started to kick but the last mermaid stopped her.

"There's something I want to show you. It's a reward for your service." She tugged on Leira's arm. "Someday you may even need it, Jasper Elf." She let go and gestured for Leira to follow and began to swim in the direction of the departing mermaids, deeper underwater. Leira looked back toward the surface again.

"The troll will wait. You're bonded. He won't leave without you," said the mermaid, turning back and swimming faster.

Leira pushed through the water but she wasn't keeping up and looked back again toward the surface. *Maybe this adventure is over.*

A whoosh of water moved around her as the mermaid returned, her tail curving around to push at Leira's back. She grabbed Leira by the arm again and pulled her along, zipping through the water past schools of colorful fish and underneath a shiver of hammerhead sharks.

The darkness intensified till all Leira could see was the hand on her arm, pulling her through the water. But it wasn't long before they were deeper and the light began to return. Only a glow at first, but then growing as they approached a way station. Leira let out a stream of bubbles in astonishment.

Below her was a platform made of leftover steel plates from sunken ships remade into something useful once again. The platform stretched out for a hundred feet and different magicals bobbed in the water just above it. In front of it were tracks laid across the ocean floor. The lights above the platform blinked twice and everyone looked to their left, leaning slightly toward the tracks.

"You have an underground railway." Leira watched, fascinated, feeling the same wonder she had felt when she first passed through a Starbucks wall.

A train car came streaking along the tracks, coming to a halt in a flash, the doors opening with a quiet whoosh, creating ripples in the water. The magicals swam onboard, some grabbing on to a metal pole as the doors closed and the train took off, moving so fast it was a streak in the water and gone again.

"You have allies down here. We know of the stories about you. If you ever need us, remember that we can get to you or help you move somewhere unseen," said the mermaid. "Our rail system connects all waterways, everywhere and is unknown to magicals who walk around up there," she said, pointing toward the surface.

Leira felt a chill roll across her back and she moved her shoulders, a spark of hope settling in her chest. "Wolfstan Humphrey doesn't know about you."

"If he's not a wet magical then no, this Wolfstan wouldn't know about us. Even the Silver Griffins up there don't know about this. But like I said, we've heard the stories and we know things are changing. You are going to need us, maybe to tip the balance in the right direction. We'll be here if that happens."

"Thank you. I'm going to tell the new Fixer, just so you know."

"Oh, the Fixers always know about us. Turner Underwood is an old friend. He told us about your partner."

"That lovely bastard is a never ending well of cool secrets."

"It takes time, but your Fixer will get to be like that too. Come on, I'll help you get back to your bonded troll."

"His name is Yumfuck and he's more of a friend. A really good one."

The mermaid circled Leira, her tail moving her through

the water. "Unless of course you want to take a ride on the train. I could get you as close as Port Arthur."

"No, I'll go back the way I came, but thank you."

The mermaid took her hand and moved her tail, pushing them through the water. "I'll have you back before you know it."

The water pushed past Leira's body as they rose toward the top, the bottom of the rusty ship tilted to one side finally coming into view.

Just before Leira emerged above the water, the mermaid stopped and pulled her back. "Blow out the water in your lungs." Leira blew out as hard as she could as the mermaid circled her head with her hand, removing the spell. She kicked to break the surface and opened her mouth wide, taking in air.

"Leira, you're back!"

Leira looked up to see the super-sized version of Yumfuck leaning over the side of the ship, his claws leaving scratch marks on the side.

The mermaid emerged, waiting as Leira climbed the anchor chain toward the top, pulling herself over the side. She looked back just in time to see the mermaid wave and flip over, her tail slapping the water.

"Are you okay?" Yumfuck looked her over, pawing the top of her wet head.

Leira pushed away his paw and gave the troll a crooked smile. "There are more wondrous things in this world than I have the ability to imagine. I think I kind of get why Turner liked being the Fixer so much. It wasn't just that he got to see so many hidden things. It was because of those things he knew the world was worth fighting for."

"That's deep." The troll smiled, showing his large, pointed teeth.

"It's like you're permanently set on comic relief."

"It's kind of my thing. Where is the Vermillion?"

"No more. He's part of the sea now."

"And the Draksa?"

"Ditto, and the mermaids lost one on their side. I'm not sure how the General will take it, but sometimes there aren't a lot of options. Let's go home."

The troll shrunk back down to five inches tall and Leira scooped him up, putting him in her wet jacket pocket. He settled in against the soggy pocket as she started the climb back down to the rocks.

"Why don't we open a portal and leave the boat?"

"Government issue. They'll want it back," said Leira, feeling an ache in her shoulders, picking her way back across the rocks. It had been a long night. "I'll open a portal once I can check that it's secure. We'll be home before you know it, Yumfuck. I'll even make you s'mores over the stove."

"Ooooh, with the big, fluffy marshmallows."

Leira grunted stepping into the boat, stretching her leg back to find her footing. "Fine, but this time you can't go to bed before you wash off the s'more."

CHAPTER TWO

Sirius sat in the mid-century leather office chair, one foot propped on the desk, pursing his lips. "I need a place to hide."

Wolfstan turned back from the window overlooking the Washington street below and arched a brow, observing Sirius. "Have you ever thought about running your family more like a business? It would appear that a lot of your trouble has been that you've let emotions rule the day. There's no accountability, no management system, no quid pro quo." He growled, glaring at the bottom of Sirius' shoe.

Sirius slowly moved his foot off the desk and sat up straighter, scowling. "I didn't come here for leadership tools. I did my best for you and now I need to go to ground and get out of the line of fire." He fanned his fingers in the air. "Live to fight another day and all."

"You did not perform as expected." Wolfstan tapped his chin with a well-manicured fingernail. "Your balance sheet shows a debt. You want my continued help, you're going to need to pay your debt."

Sirius let out an exasperated sigh, adjusting his cashmere coat. "I have a feeling this will be a far greater assignment than any debt."

"It's all subjective." Wolfstan's expression grew cold. "I need you to bring me a few magicals. A baker's dozen should do."

"What do you want with magicals?" Sirius swallowed hard, feeling his stomach sour.

"I'm advancing the fight for magicals everywhere before the gates open completely." Wolfstan tilted his head slightly. "But in order to get to the destination, a few volunteers will be needed to further the cause."

"I've heard about this place." Sirius twirled a finger in the air. "You're doing some kind of Frankenstein experiments."

Wolfstan pounded on the desktop and ran a fingernail noisily across the wood leaving a slight scratch. "I am promulgating science and making sure of our place here on this world. My duty is to lead us there. Yours is to get what I need or die trying."

Sirius felt a chill across the back of his neck, magic humming through his arms the way it always did when he was in dire straits. But this time he knew better than to move a muscle.

"There's a particular magical I want, Sirius. A shifter that you created. An alpha who has settled here named Matthew Moss. His genetics may hold the key for me to figuring out how to make everything work together."

"That should be easy enough." Sirius curled his lip. "Shifters aren't really magicals."

Wolfstan let out a sharp laugh. "Jealousy is always ugly.

Just because they've formed an alliance with your replacements, don't get your feelings hurt." Wolfstan tapped the desk again. "Don't be lazy this time and underestimate your adversary. My assistant has something for you that may help. An ointment we've developed that will destabilize their DNA. Use it judiciously and test it once or twice. Matthew Moss runs with his pack most nights through Rock Creek Park. Usually around midnight they transform back to their human selves to head home. That will be his most vulnerable moment. Don't fail me, Sirius. Or you will have to find a place to hide from me."

"And if I bring you the magicals you need? I may have a sister I'll throw in as a bonus."

"Then I will help you to find a new identity that will be undetectable to everyone. Trust me, you'll love it."

Sirius felt the sense of dread settle in and take hold of him deep inside. "I'll see what I can do," he said, earning a smile from Wolfstan that made the chill blow back across his neck.

CHAPTER THREE

Correk and Leira sat across the kitchen table from Lily. "You think you have it?" asked Leira.

"She has to *believe* she has it," said Correk. "She has to know it."

Lily licked her lips and gave a slight nod. "I have it. I'm sure of it. I'm very good at spells. I always have been." The words spilled out of her in a rush.

"That's the first time a Fixer spell has been given to someone outside the... the line." Correk's brow was furrowed, studying Lily.

Lily nervously nodded again. "I'm honored." She shifted in her chair, straightening up. "I can do this, you know. I'm sure of it. I come from a long line of warrior witches."

Leira reached over and squeezed the young witch's hand. "Damn right you do. You're also very brave."

Lily blinked, startled. "You're the one who always runs toward trouble. I'm creeping toward it."

Leira gave a slight smile. "I'd say you're more like a fast

walk. Just shows you're also very smart to gather enough information, first."

"You have the artifact?" asked Correk, leaning across the table. "It'll be necessary to boost your magic enough to pull off the ancient spell."

Lily held up the blue marble, a light twinkling inside of it like a miniature summer storm.

"Louie comes in handy at just the right moments. Have you ever noticed that?" Leira looked closer, admiring the marble. She sat back and reached out her hands. "We're agreed on the plan?"

Each of them took a hand. "Lily gets her research and stays as long as she can," said Correk.

"Or until things go completely to hell," said Leira.

"Whichever comes first," said Lily, her voice cracking, still lifting her chin. "And before I leave, I infect the project and get the hell out of there without Wolfstan knowing his pet project has gone south. I can do this."

"Remember, the spell can be unstable and will only last a few minutes, long enough for you to get in and do what you need to do. Don't dawdle," said Correk. "Get back to your workstation as fast as possible."

"Understood. I will do the best I can."

Please let that be enough, thought Leira, smiling at Lily.

Lily sat in front of her station at the long table, looking through the microscope. *It works. It really works. Another piece of the puzzle.* She sat up and glanced to her right. The biologists around her were bent over looking at slides.

No one looked up to notice Lily's gobsmacked expression.

Despite the row of people huddled in the lab, the only sound in the room was the hum from the air filtration system. Lily took in a deep breath and let it out slowly, leaning back over and taking another look just to be sure. *Still there.* The cells were altering into something completely new and reforming themselves. Something magical was mutating.

A microscopic flash of purple lightning startled Lily and the cells disappeared for a moment in a shadow that was there and then it was gone. *Was that a glitch? I can't be sure.*

Lily pressed her lips together and put her hands on the metal table, willing herself to remain calm. *No, it's time. Time for part two of this plan. You can do this, Lily.*

She picked up an old slide and deftly slid it into place, taking out the other slide and palming it in her hand.

"I'm going to get something from the vending machines. You want something?" she whispered to Claire who was hunched over her microscope.

"What? No, I'm good." Claire bit her lip and typed notes into her iPad. "Seems like a lot of trouble for some Sun chips. It'll be lunch in a couple of hours."

Lily bit the inside of her cheek. "Yeah, well, no one wants to see me hangry. Maybe I'll get two bags to make it worth the trip." She typed with one hand, locking her iPad and headed for the door.

"Hey, I'll take a Snickers," called out Billy.

"Yeah, I'll see what I can do," said Lily, as Claire let out a snort.

Lily walked slowly out the first set of doors, the quiet whoosh behind her as they closed. She took off the booties and protective equipment, wrapping the slide in them and pushing it all down in the bin.

She grabbed her purse and walked closer to the second set of doors, the scanner reading the chip in her arm as they opened with another soft *whoosh.* She slipped the strap of her purse on her shoulder and pulled out her wand, looking around to make sure she was alone. She tapped the tip against the chip, putting her in the ladies' room on the log and kept walking, picking up just enough speed to look like she was late to something important. No time to talk to anyone she might pass in the corridors.

She looked down slightly and kept walking, ducking into a stairwell and waving her wand again to make her image fade from the cameras. At the railing she looked up through the middle of the stairs and then down below and hesitated. *You're already in too deep, Lily. You can't go back. Not and live with yourself.* She stood up straighter and squared her shoulders, glancing at her watch. She had five, maybe ten minutes before it would look like she had a problem in the ladies' room. She couldn't afford to have anything strange on the employee reports.

Wolfstan Humphrey was bound to be looking for irregularities.

She took off up the stairs heading to the tenth floor to see for herself what they were doing. Part two of the plan. It wasn't long before she was at the metal door with a large ten painted on the wall next to it. She reached into her purse and pulled out the post-it with the spell written on it. Just in case.

"For us, nothing is spared, nothing is sealed, nothing is unknown," she muttered, glancing at it and putting the paper away. She held up her hands, shaking slightly and practiced the symbols exactly as Correk had shown her at the kitchen table. Blowing out a breath, she shook off the feeling of danger that clung to her these days. "Time to put the two together," she whispered. She started the symbols and began speaking. "For us, nothing is spared, nothing is sealed, nothing is unknown."

Lily watched in astonishment as the air around her rippled and the door opened with a soft click. The young witch pulled it open and slipped through, her eyes growing wide at what she saw. She looked down at her watch and saw that the seconds had stopped spinning past.

People were motionless, frozen at the last thing they were doing before the spell took hold. The air around them was performing the same ripple and the only sound was a high-pitched sustained whistle. Objects hung in the air and a falling pen was halfway to the floor. Time was holding still.

Lily slipped around the different bodies, taking note of the different large metal vats holding live animals with artifacts implanted in different places. Some were standing, attached to a variety of colored tubes. Others were laid out on large examining tables with scientists bent over them, making notes.

There was an ache in Lily's chest, and she brushed her hand lightly against the fur of the closest animal, her fingers lingering over the red kill button. Her eyes were shining as she kept moving, only a few minutes left. *Stick to the plan.*

She went to the closest computer and held up the arm of the biologist to line up the chip, gaining access to the mainframe. "Come on, come on, come on." The folders on the desktop scrolled past until she found the one she needed. She opened it, scrolling to the lines of code two thirds of the way down. She licked her dry lips and swallowed, typing as fast as she could to change just a few parts of the code. "Just enough to ensure failure."

The pulses in the air flickered and Lily felt her heart quicken, closing the folder and putting the screen back to where it was as she reversed her steps, running back through the lab toward the stairs. "Someday I'll come back and make this right," she whispered, a shudder passing down her back as she took a look back, the door shutting with a click. Her watch clicked forward as time resumed and the whine in the air disappeared.

Lily went to the stairs and took them two at a time, her hand brushing along the handrail till she got back to her floor, moving as fast as she could toward the snack machine. She tapped her arm with her wand, resetting her chip to put her by the snack machine and slid in her card, getting two bags of Sun chips. She pushed the buttons again and threw in a Snickers for good luck.

CHAPTER FOUR

"You've been working a lot lately." Correk was standing in their bedroom. He was watching Leira get dressed, letting himself feel the flow of magical energy slipping around him from all over the world. He was paying attention to both things at once.

"Look who's talking. I can tell you're doing that vibe thing, dipping into the stream."

"I don't dip into it as much as pay attention for a second. It's always there."

Leira stopped for a moment and gave him a longer look. "Then how do you pay attention to anything else?"

"You learn."

"It's like you're never alone."

"I take it General Anderson called again. It's becoming a regular thing. Almost like you work for him again. Where are you headed this time?"

"Not General Anderson. Private commission. Apparently my reputation is growing among certain circles. A wizard has taken over a corner of New York City and is peddling drugs back to the humans. I'm surprised this hasn't happened sooner."

"It has and often, but the Silver Griffins always took care of it. You're moving in on their territory."

"I've been traveling through their territory for some time. This one is unique because he also got hold of an artifact from the Silver Griffin's old vault. A very powerful artifact. It helps its magical owner hear from a distance, even through wards."

Correk arched an eyebrow, a scowl growing across his face. "Only a Silver Griffin could have gotten an artifact from that vault."

Leira pulled on a boot. "I know. That's why I took the job. There's a traitor in the mix and that artifact could also lead us to a name. Maybe that will help Lois stop being so mad at us."

"Lily is safe for today," said Correk, clearing his throat.

"We've slowed Wolfstan down for half a second. She can stay under the radar at least till I get back from the job. Plus, I'm getting paid a shit load of money. We could, imagine this..." she said, holding up her hands, "get new appliances. Yeah? A working kitchen," she whispered into his ear, gently biting his ear lobe before bending down to get her other boot.

"How do you know your contact is legit?"

"I'm not new to this." She pulled on her boot and pursed her lips. "And I checked him out on the magicals version of the dark web. He's been a pain in their ass for some time." Leira stomped her foot, adjusting the fit of the boot. "They're calling me a bounty hunter on their site." She smiled, slipping into the leather jacket Turner made for her. "I could get used to that."

"What are you going to do with him once you catch him?"

"My instructions are to get back the artifact and leave him with Lois. The artifact is to go to Turner Underwood. He's the one who introduced us over the phone." She watched Correk's eyebrow rise. "I trust Turner," she said, "and besides, someone has to get that artifact off the street. Might as well be me. Bounty hunter."

"What's this guy's name?"

"He goes by Doc Leahy, but his origins are in question. Get this, Doc is sending along a chopper to help locate the wizard. Big money brings big toys." She opened her hand, pulling in energy, her eyes glowing. A ball of light appeared and she pulled it apart, opening a portal to a noisy city street. "But I have a feeling Turner knows all about him. Play nice with Yumfuck while I'm gone." Leira stepped through, pushing against the sides.

"One of these days I'm going to figure out how he keeps finding my stash."

"Then what will you do with your spare time?" she asked, pulling in her arms and blowing a kiss as the portal closed. Sparks danced along the broken asphalt between the brick buildings.

Leira crouched in the darkness beside an old eight-story building on the outskirts of Alphabet City in the Lower East Side of Manhattan. She checked the coordinates and could see she was two buildings away from the target. Close enough for the artifact to pick up on her approach. Leira pulled out her phone and called the number she'd been given as the sound of a helicopter grew nearer.

"You're on headset," said the pilot.

"Shine on 7th and Avenue D. Second building in. Our target is inside. Be looking for a tall male with long brown hair and a dark tattoo on his right hand."

"Roger that."

The helicopter soon was right overhead, the light directed just across the street, away from the correct building.

"Sometimes I really love my job."

Leira had lied to the pilot, knowing the target would be listening. The description of the wizard was accurate, but it was the wrong address. Still, close enough to make it look legitimate. *Just the beginning, pal.*

Prancing through the front doors wasn't going to work, especially if anyone spotted her and opened their mouth to say something to her. He would hear it and create a portal to pop through.

Going to have to be smart about this one.

She looked at the old metal fire escape that hung on the side of the building. Luckily for Leira, it was an old walk up and still had a fire escape, even if it was one of the tallest left at eight stories. But managing it without making any noise was going to be interesting.

She rubbed her hands together, ready to test how much running was about to pay off. *Just like the old days. Maybe I'll even use my zip-ties and handcuff him old-school.*

Leira waited till the chopper made a slow circle overhead, the noise growing gradually louder till it was overhead. She slowly pulled the ladder down and leaned against the building for a moment to make sure no one was coming out to take a look. She started to climb, stepping carefully on the edge of each step and across each platform to keep the creaks and groans of the old rusty metal to a minimum.

A window opened above her when she'd reached the sixth floor. She flattened herself against the wall and peered through the spaces in the landing above as a wizard with a buzz cut and a bent nose leaned out the window and looked around the alley. Not the target.

"There's nothing there, Mule. Must have been rats. Those things are meat eaters. Some of them are as big as Willens." He pulled himself back inside and slid the window shut as Leira started up the last two flights.

Mule. He's in there. Sweet. She got to the last platform and inched along the wall, waiting for the chopper to take another pass overhead, drowning out any other sounds.

Leira drew in just enough energy as a small orb of light lifted from her palm and skittered over the building acting as a GPS in case the wizard went old school on her too.

A faint glow appeared down her arms and she read the symbols flipping across her skin. No wards. Not so smart.

Leira took a deep breath, closed her eyes, and drew more light through her body. The landing began to shake, clinking and clacking against the side of the brick building, a fine mist of dust gathering in the air. The magicals inside were reacting to the commotion when a flunky lifted the window poking out his head.

Leira swiftly kicked him square in the jaw and dove through the window, using him as a shield. The target lifted his wand, striking his compatriot in the chest, burning a two inch hole as Leira pushed forward, throwing the hefty wizard at two others who easily dodged their falling comrade.

Leira fanned out her hands, spitting out a volley of small fireballs that attached themselves like barbs to the two magicals who patted themselves down, yowling like feral cats.

Mule headed for the window, diving headfirst and clutching the artifact under his arm.

"Oh, hell no, you don't." Leira quickly followed him and looked over the edge of the fire escape. The wizard looked up and smirked, sending a spray of fire directly at her face. She leaned back, the shot barely missing her, hitting the bricks off to the side.

Mule leapt downstairs, surprising Leira and exchanging fireballs with her. Just as she reached the third floor, his feet hit the alley. She hurried on to the ground as something slammed against her chest, picked her up, and threw her into the side of the building. She shook her head as her body slowly absorbed the pulse of magic.

"Ouch, asshole," she gasped, sucking air back into her lungs. She felt the pain against her joints from the pressurized spell.

She rocked on to her feet and sprinted after the wizard, watching him turn left out of the side alley onto 8th Avenue.

Leira picked up the pace, cutting the distance between them and skidded around the corner with one hand grazing the rough brick of the nearby wall.

"Son of a..." She ducked at the last moment, a fireball zipping over her head. She started running after him again, calculating the point where she would finally catch him. Mule reached Avenue A, dodging a taxi and almost getting hit by a scooter, the artifact pressed against his chest.

She reached the intersection just as the wizard glanced over his shoulder and took off into the traffic, swirling his wand to move the cars around him. Leira jumped off the curb as he reached the other side and canceled his spell. The cars corrected and raced toward her, then turning their wheels again to avoid hitting her even as she kept moving.

Horns honked loudly, and tires screeched as she leapt onto a taxi hood and jumped off the other side. She saw the fear and wide eyes of the drivers, quickly replaced by annoyance when they missed her. No need to worry about explanations at least. *Love New Yorkers.*

By the time she had made it across Mule was already at the entrance of Tompkins Square Park.

Leira followed, continuing to gain ground on him, throwing several balls of light at his head that popped and fizzled when they got to their mark, clouding Mule's sight. He growled, swirling his wand in front of his face as he crossed the wide grey pavers, bounding over the waist-high iron fence, one hand on the railing.

He ducked under the trees and was out of Leira's line of sight for a few seconds. But it didn't take long before sparks of green and blue shot out from under the trees. They were followed by torpedoes made of thrumming light emitting a steady whine, splitting into smaller missiles and circling around behind her, flying over a man sleeping on a nearby bench.

Leira managed to dodge most of them, using the

stream of magic trailing behind her to act like a net, slinging them back at Mule. A new trick courtesy of Turner Underwood.

One torpedo found her and slammed into the back of her right knee, pushing her to the ground.

She felt her knee bang against the slate pavers and gritted her teeth, making herself get up in one fluid motion and keep moving, vaulting over the fence.

The magic was flowing through her making her reflexes pick up speed. She took in each sound just ahead of her, picking out the ones that belonged to Mule, stumbling over tree roots, still trying to get away.

"Got you," she whispered, letting the magic guide her.

Mule yelled when she tackled him, and they rolled to a stop with Leira above him, her knee pressing hard against his diaphragm. She snatched his wand from his hand and held a ball of fire just above his face.

"I don't usually complain about a woman being on top, but do you mind?" He sneered and tried reaching for his wand, laying back defeated with his eyebrows singed.

Leira growled, narrowing her eyes and pressing the solid piece of hickory against his throat. "I would be careful who you talk to like that. I don't need a wand to send your ass to the next world. They asked me to bring you back, but they didn't specify whether you had to be breathing for me to collect."

The helicopter circled overhead, shining the spotlight on the two of them. Leira shaded her eyes as she glanced up and waved her arm for the all clear.

"You gave them the wrong information on purpose," he choked out. "Well done."

"You aren't the brightest. That's not even the most clever thing I've done today. Where's the artifact?"

"I don't know what you mean."

"Seriously, dude? Respect for being trapped like an ant under a magnifier at high noon and still thinking lying is a good option." Leira pressed the wand more firmly against his neck, the fireball still blazing in her other hand. "But quit dicking around. Where is the damn artifact."?

The wizard grimaced and tried kicking out his legs but Leira lowered the fireball, turning his nose a slight red.

"Are you done yet?"

He let out a resigned sigh and laid back, flopping his arms out to the side. "Behind the tree." He lifted his chin and looked back as far as he could. "That elm."

Leira closed her hand over the fireball, snuffing it out and rolled Mule over, zip tying his hands together. "Move and I'll take it personally, Mule. That won't go well for you."

She darted behind the elm and found the cloth sack, coming back to kneel beside the defeated wizard. "Was this thing really worth this much trouble?" She reached in and pulled out a ten inch brass ear trumpet, slightly dented. She held the narrow end up closer to her ear and heard a hundred conversations piled on top of each other. Slowly, her energy connected with each one, pulling out the words till she found one between a mother and a young boy that caught her attention. Then all the other voices dropped away. Leira's expression softened listening to the small boy's voice.

"I think Super Mario is hungry."

"Your little brother's name is Edward."

"No, that won't work. Super Mario is better."

Mule jerked his head up, trying to nudge Leira. "What will happen to me now?"

Leira lowered the artifact and slipped it back into its bag. "You'll get to meet some nice suburban Moms."

Mule groaned and put his face against the grass. "Not the Silver Griffins. They have no sense of humor."

"I don't know. You catch them on a good day."

"What if I make you a deal? I could tell you about some other artifacts and help you with an even bigger score. I'm really just a little fish."

"Tempting, but you're on my work order so for today, you'll have to do. Maybe you can try that same deal with the Silver Griffins and see how far you get." She grabbed Mule by the arm and helped him to his feet, a ball of light forming in her other hand and the bag dangling from her wrist by the drawstrings. "Time to go, Mule." Leira let go of him to pull the ball apart and he tried to start running but Leira easily put out her foot and tripped him. "Timber!"

The portal opened to the address she had been given for when the assignment was complete. Two witches were waiting on the other side, their wands drawn and pointed at the pair. Leira leaned down and grabbed Mule under his arms, dragging him through the portal.

"What if I could tell you about where the drug supply is being stashed." The portal closed behind them, sparks hitting the bottom of Mule's shoes.

"Ooof, lay off the cupcakes, Mule. Again, that's a great bargaining chip with the Silver Griffins. You and I are about to part company and I'm going to head out." She rolled Mule toward the two agents and gave them a nod. "He's all yours now."

"Come on, Mule. We have a nice warm cell waiting for you."

The other witch looked at her phone. "I need to get back and get the kids' lunches made for tomorrow. Let's get a move on."

Leira gave a crooked smile and opened another portal to the dark side of Turner Underwood's large house. "Ladies. Mule." She stepped in and quickly pulled the portal shut, heading around the side of the house and going up to the door, using her key to let herself inside.

"Turner's not here."

Leira startled and stopped in her tracks, pulling the artifact closer. In the dim light from a streetlamp near a window she could see a woman in a dress with a high collar and a tight waist that hung all the way to the floor. Her hair was loosely gathered on top of her head, ending in a soft bun with a ribbon tied around it.

"You're from Turner's small city." Leira furrowed her brow, taking in every detail.

"I'm a refugee from Oriceran, yes. Turner asked me to wait here for you and tell you to leave the artifact in the safe in his office at the end of this hall. He said to tell you the combination is the troll's birthday plus his age."

The corners of Leira's mouth curled up and she stepped forward, still keeping an eye on the woman. "You're an Elf?"

"Light Elf, yes. My name is Winland."

"Turner must think a lot of you to let you play go

between." Leira passed by her, glancing down at the pointed boots with buttons up the sides.

"I would hope so. I'm his daughter."

Leira stopped and swiveled on her heel, trying to take in the information. "Daughter? Turner has a kid... a grown Elf daughter?"

"You've met my father. I have a few brothers and sisters and they all have their own mothers."

Leira grimaced. "That does kind of track. Wow, he does like to play things close to the vest."

"You're Leira Berens. He talks about you all the time. More than he talks about all of us." She put up her long, slender hand. "It's alright. It's actually safer that way. Can you imagine if magicals learned Turner Underwood had a family? We'd always be at risk."

Leira felt a slight chill go down her back, thinking of Correk and their future. "Makes sense. Nice to meet you, Winland." She turned back and bit her lip but asked the question anyway. "You said you're a refugee. That would mean your mother..."

"Was a follower of Rhazdon, yes." Winland held Leira's gaze without looking away, reminding Leira a little of Turner. "We are all capable of great mistakes. You see my father as some great magical because of the spells he can do. But his real magic is his ability to see into people's hearts and look past those mistakes."

"Winland, I hope I get to know you better."

"There's time, a lot of it. I'll be here for a while, too."

"Then I'll be back to hear your story. I need to get this artifact tucked away and get home before I'm missed."

Leira slowly turned and headed for the study at the end of the hall. "I really need to go see Jackson," she muttered.

She easily found the safe and set the dial for twelve, then twenty-five, and then two. It was the date Leira had given Yumfuck for his birthday plus their years together. The troll was fond of saying his life really began when he bonded with Leira.

The safe made a distinct click when she pulled on the handle, opening the heavy green door. She slid the artifact inside on top of folders, only tempted for a moment to look at them. There was a hum of energy coming off them that pushed at Leira's hand. "They've gotta be booby trapped. I'd be disappointed if they weren't." Her hand wavered over the top. "Nope, not going home with bright green skin tonight." She shook her head and closed the safe, pushing the handle back up till it clicked again.

When Leira went back out into the hallway Winland was gone and the public side of the house felt empty. "I'll bet you have a great story to tell Winland Underwood," said Leira, heading toward the front door. Definitely coming back."

CHAPTER FIVE

*C*ome over for coffee in the morning! I want you to meet a couple of my friends. It'll be fun.

Leira got the text just as she walked into the kitchen and glanced at the time. *Way past midnight. Angel is still up.* Correk came walking into the room holding a pile of empty Cheetos bags in his arms, an eyebrow arched. "I told you he was raiding my stash."

"That was never in doubt and you still don't know how he's doing it. Nice to see you too." Leira laughed and sat down in the nearest chair.

"Everything turn out okay?"

"You already know it did. I know you check in on my magical stream just like everyone else's. I'd complain but it's kind of hot."

Correk kissed the top of her head and dropped the evidence on the kitchen table. "You say that about everything I do."

"All true."

"Who's texting you?"

Leira glanced out the window at the lights next door. "Angel Moss. She wants me to come by for coffee tomorrow. A coffee klatch with her friends."

"That scares you more than taking down the wizard, doesn't it?" Correk chuckled and sat down next to her, putting his arm around her waist.

Leira rested her head on his shoulder. "You do know me." She let out a sigh. "I have to go. We need to try and be some kind of normal in between danger and mayhem."

"Names of our future children."

Leira suddenly sat up and turned to look at Correk. "You'll never guess who I met tonight. Winland Underwood. That's right, relative of Turner's. His daughter and apparently not his only offspring. Wait, you don't look surprised. You knew!"

"Turner swore me to secrecy, even from you."

"I suppose I shouldn't be insulted. Wow, first time I'm really getting there are already secrets floating around in your head. Hmmm, that's hot."

"Let's go to bed," he said, getting up slowly, taking her by the hand.

"Very good idea. I could use a shower first."

"Want company?"

"Always."

Leira stood at Angel's door, practicing looking casual and glad to be there. She opened and closed her hands, shaking them out at her sides, leaning back to see if Correk or the troll were watching her from next door. She was in the middle of doing her best stink eye aimed at her house when the Moss front door opened and Angel came bursting out, enveloping Leira in a hug.

"Oh, okay, sure." Leira patted Angel's back, still feeling her shoulders relaxing into it. "It's like you have your own magic," muttered Leira.

"What?" Angel stepped back, ushering Leira into the door, already onto the next thing. "Come meet my friends. You'll love them! Norah runs a nonprofit to teach the arts to children..." Angel pointed toward a young woman with a pale complexion and short blonde hair with bangs that swept across her forehead wearing tight black pants and a long blouse. Norah gave a wave, taking a sip of her wine. "Over there is Nicole who does commercial real estate and Celeste is in human resources for a large corporation."

Nicole had dark braids that cascaded down her back and rosy brown skin. She came gliding over, already talking about the neighborhood and welcoming Leira. Celeste hung back, tilting her head and watching the others, her dark hair fanning across one shoulder.

"Have you been to any of the museums yet? Of course there's the Air and Space museum," said Nicole, not waiting for an answer. "Do you have kids? There's the International Spy Museum or the Smithsonian Castle."

Leira shook her head no, looking back and forth between Nicole and Angel.

"And the Freer is great," chirped Angel. "Do you want a glass of wine? I have a chardonnay from that same vineyard the waiter gave us or a sparkling rosé. What was it called Norah?"

"La Fete du Rosé. All the way from France."

"There's a tres leches cake from Bread Bite Bakery. Celeste brought it," said Angel, gently nudging Leira further into the room.

"My favorite thing to eat," said Celeste, smiling and leaning forward. "Angel said we needed to make a good impression, so you'd agree to be our fourth Musketeer."

Leira felt her cheeks warm and she opened and shut her mouth several times trying to find something to say. "Rosé," was all that came out. *No swearing. Correk said no swearing. Fuck.*

"I also said to not say that part when she was still at the front door," laughed Angel. "But you've hunted down killers. I promise we're a lot easier than that."

Leira took the glass of wine and sat down next to Nicole, admiring the silver rings that lined her fingers. "Those are beautiful. They look handmade."

"They are and I'm the one who made them. It's my hobby and the way I blow off steam."

"That's quite the hobby," said Leira. "Mine is trying to renovate our house."

"Oooh, that doesn't count as a hobby," said Norah. "A hobby has to be fun, so renovating is already out, and can't be for profit or a have-to."

"Basically, your job, Norah," laughed Celeste.

"Truth! But I love what I do."

"Someday I may turn this hobby into my profession," said Nicole, fanning out her fingers. "But right now, the siren song of commercial real estate has me in its grip." She winked at Leira. "Too much moola to walk away. Maybe after the kids are grown." She pulled out her phone and showed two tall skinny boys and a little girl leaning against the taller one, sticking out her tongue. "That's Alicia. She is going to either be the CEO of something big or a Nascar driver. She's always moving and always thinking. Last week," she said, scrolling through her pictures, "she was outside for five minutes and came to the door looking like this." Nicole held up an image of the little girl painted blue and only wearing her underwear, also blue. "Alicia figured out that chalk will dissolve in puddles."

"She looks like a smurf." Celeste leaned over to get a better look. "Didn't she take apart your microwave last month?"

"She did and Joe and I were in the house and heard nothing." Nicole smiled and shook her head, slipping her phone back into her purse. "I still say her brothers were covering for her. It makes me happy that they're a team and scares the crap out of me that they're a team."

Angel laughed and held up her hand as Nicole high-fived her.

Leira grinned watching all the women work like puzzle pieces with each other, fitting together just right.

"Time for cake," said Celeste. "Leira you've been here long enough to at least be lukewarm and I'm starving. By the way wine and cake is our idea of brunch."

The three women paused, looking at Leira.

"Fucking right it is!" Leira gave them a crooked smile, a hand on her hip. The women broke into a cheer, Norah letting out a loud whoop.

"I like her," said Nicole, pointing a finger at Leira and laughing. "I have to limit cussing to the car when the kids aren't around, so they don't tell their teachers."

"They're like little sponges," said Celeste. "I have two

girls, eight and ten and they repeat anything that will get them a laugh or make them look cool. They're also small spies that take all my money."

"I'm divorced and my kids are all at work," said Norah. "That's where I get my fix."

"You guys are doing a great job of selling motherhood," said Angel, taking a long sip of wine.

"Hey, I did it three times. That should tell you something." Nicole threw up her hands, sloshing her wine.

"Watch the floors."

"Watch the wine, hell with the floors," said Nicole. "No offense." She patted Angel's back.

"I'd be offended but I'm usually the one spilling it." Angel pulled a long knife out of a wooden block, deftly slicing the cake and sliding pieces onto glass plates and passing them down the line.

Norah added a fork as each plate went by her. Leira took a bite of the cold, moist cake and felt it melt in her mouth. "My mother used to make this all the time when I was little. I forgot how good it is."

"What made her stop?" Nicole ignored the frowns from the other women, making Leira smile.

"Life took some strange turns and now she's a newlywed and has better things to do."

"Ooooh, damn right she does," said Norah, laughing.

Leira smiled again and took another bite. *I'm gonna like this neighborhood.*

CHAPTER SIX

Harkin held the bowl in his hand, letting his magic connect to it. He completed the circuit, letting the blend pass through the electronics from the machine and connect to a sample of some of Peyton's cells. He watched, fascinated as the cells morphed and changed, giving off purple sparks until they settled into a new configuration. His head jerked back involuntarily, a look of confusion on his face. "Is it possible?" he muttered.

Harkin pulled out a dropper and put more cells onto a slide, repeating the process. Again, the cells began vibrating, shaking and moving around as they became something new. "Repaired themselves," Harkin said breathlessly. He tried it again and again and again with the same results, his heart beating faster and faster.

A rush of energy coursed through him and his mind swam as he forced himself to focus. He looked back again, his chest tight, doing his best to let go of the strange feeling of hope.

"It's the same! I'm sure of it." He slowly pulled out the old slide of Peyton's DNA Harkin had carefully preserved and carefully slid it into place, his fingers tingling. One slide sat just above the other as he looked through the lens. He swallowed hard, his hands trembling. "The same," he whispered. "It worked. The cells have regenerated themselves into the original form."

Harkin looked at the ancient bowl. "Where did you come from? And can you heal Peyton? Someone in the dark families has a piece of the puzzle."

Leira pushed open the screen door and came into the laboratory with Hagan right behind her. "That's good and bad news. I stopped by to say hello to Hagan and wanted to check on you."

Hagan was balancing a charcoal grey box with Astro Doughnuts in small white type on the side. In his other hand was a square donut with a bite missing. "Maple bacon, can you believe it? And square! Tastes the same as the round ones. You want one? There's an Old Bay donut I'm willing to part with."

"You haven't even tried it. You might regret that. It came with a high recommendation, and you're welcome."

"I already said thank you three times."

"This place looks almost exactly the same as the setup you had on Oriceran." Leira glanced toward the glass front bookcase where Peyton's cell had been on Oriceran. "Almost."

Harkin ignored the comment, glancing back at the cells. *Still there. All these years. Is it possible?* "It was the Gardener's idea." His brain spun through the possibilities and he was gently holding the bowl close to his body. "He said it would be more efficient."

"Man, are you okay?" Hagan went closer to Harkin, his eyes narrowing, looking him over. "You don't look like yourself."

Harkin's eyes were shining, words sputtering out of him. Leira came and gently put a hand on his shoulder and Harkin felt the low hum of her magic, always there at the surface. "What's happened, Harkin? Should we get Correk?"

Harkin snapped out of it at the sound of his son's name. "No, no that won't be necessary." He held the bowl closer to his chest. "I think I have the answer to help Peyton," he whispered. "I've waited a hundred years to say those words. It's the bowl. Someone in the dark family figured part of this out before." Harkin held the bowl closer, leaning toward Leira. "You have to take me to him. We have to try. I can fix him." His chest was rising and falling.

"I can see that this matters to you a lot, but we can't be sure of what will happen, and Peyton has already been through a lot." Leira felt Harkin's pain pass through her, mixed with a new and fragile sense of joy.

"I'm sure. I am sure. Look! Look at the cells. They regenerated. I've repeated the experiment over and over again and it's always exactly the same."

"Do you know how the bowl is doing it?"

Harkin shook his head, still excited, "I have no idea. We'll need to find out the origins of the bowl. Maybe it will lead us to the spell and the magical. But for now..." He stopped talking, a tear sliding down his cheek. "I can help Peyton and calm his magic, heal his brain."

"That sounds like a tall order." Hagan rolled his eyes, adjusting his pants. "Maybe the Gardener and Correk should be in on the decision."

Harkin carefully laid the bowl on the work surface, sliding it away from the edge. He grabbed hold of Leira's arm, his eyes glowing as he let his magic surge, combining with her light and making her bracelet jangle. "Please. I know this will work. When I tried before I was in a rush just trying to save his life. There was no time. But I've had all the time in the world to work on the solution and this bowl is giving him a chance."

"You sure it's not about you?" asked Hagan, drumming his sticky fingers on the counter. Harkin scowled at him and he stopped. "Sorry. But the question still stands."

"It's a fair question, Harkin." Leira's eyes glowed from the magic roiling around between them.

Harkin looked out the window at the trees in the Texas sanctuary. "Part of it is about me. I caused it. I started all of this. Would Wolfstan even be trying to take over two worlds if I hadn't told him about my experiments?"

"Hard yes. He would have tried another way. I think that one was a foregone conclusion," said Leira. "You were the convenience."

Harkin let go of Leira and let the magic subside. "Peyton was... is my best friend. This is still mostly about him. He has a lot of life left as an Elf if I can fix this."

Leira pursed her lips. "If Turner, Correk and the Gardener are on board, then we try. It can't just be up to me or you. Till then, take good care of that bowl and I'll see what I can do about finding its original owner. One more thing to get out of Sirius."

"Can I at least see Peyton. See that he's alright?"

Leira glanced at Hagan who shrugged. "That's your call, Berens." Hagan took out another donut and chomped down. "Hey, a PB&J. Not bad," he said, licking jelly off his lip as some slid down his chin.

"It's hard to take you seriously when you're doing that."

"Rose says the same thing. That's alright, no one was asking you to."

Leira gave a crooked smile. "You haven't changed at all."

"Is that a yes?" Harkin arched a brow, and Leira noticed again how much Correk looked like his father at times.

She let out a sigh and held up her hands. "Yes, that's a yes, but the bowl stays here. I want your word. You don't try any noble gestures until everyone's on board. And you say nothing about any of this to Peyton. Do we have a deal?"

A shudder passed through Harkin. "We have a deal."

Harkin waited in Turner Underwood's study pacing back and forth. Leira wouldn't let him go with her to retrieve Peyton. She wouldn't even tell him where it was in the large house. "I gave my word," she had said, shutting the study door with a click.

After a while the door finally opened again and Leira led in the tall Light Elf wearing a narrow cut dark suit. Stray strands of broken light occasionally flashed around his face and hands, making him twitch sporadically. "You can see the magic is mostly under control as long as he's under this roof," said Leira, keeping a hand on Peyton's back, helping to control the energy levels while he was out of the inner world of the city. His magic would pass through her, smooth and silky and then abruptly break, sending a sharp sting. Leira looked up at Peyton and bit her lip. "You're doing great."

Harkin rushed forward but Leira held up her hand. "Give him some space. He may not understand much but he knows enough not to associate you with good times in his life.

"Correk said someone would always know where they stood with you. Why is he dressed like that?"

"Too long of a story. You don't have long. Say what you need to say and then you'll need to go back to the sanctuary."

Harkin's jaw worked from side to side. "I'm glad you're doing better," he finally said. "I've made a lot of mistakes that have hurt you over and over again." He shook his head as Peyton let out a low level growl. "I'm not going to apologize again. I've done that too many times and it added up to nothing." He licked his lips nervously as Leira shook her head hard and scowled at him. He cleared his throat. "I'll see you again, Peyton. Maybe in better times."

Leira's expression softened and she led Peyton back toward the door, glancing over her shoulder at Harkin. "I'm glad you're back, Harkin. Come by for dinner this week. I promise not to cook, and we can show you around the neighborhood. Okay?"

"I'd like that." He watched the small light flashes around the back of Peyton's neck.

"Good. I might even see if I can find Jackson and get him to make an appearance."

"Leira... thank you."

She looked back again. "Of course. It's what family does for each other," she said, pulling the door shut behind her.

CHAPTER SEVEN

"Here's where I put your new candy stash." Lois pointed to a drawer in the plain wooden desk before pushing her glasses up her nose. "Of course, that's if you choose to join the Silver Griffins." Lois crossed her fingers behind her back, smiling at Patsy.

"I know you have your fingers crossed. I know you better than Earle knows you." Patsy held up her hand before Lois could interrupt. "We both know it's true. I'm not sure I want to work for you. I'm used to working with you."

"We could give you a special title. Go ahead, open the drawer."

"Like what? Could I be a duchess? That would be fun."

Lois rolled her eyes. "Sure. Duchess Patsy working on special operations." She slowly slipped her wand out of her pocket, watching Patsy inspect the room, making a point of ignoring the desk. Lois gave a small jerk to her wand, spitting fire spitballs at Patsy, zinging her.

"Ow! Hey! Your pants aren't so big I can't still zing you

back." Patsy licked her hand and rubbed the pink mark on her arm. "That last one hurt. You must be getting sore. Fine, I'll look at the candy stash. What, did you pull out all the green ones for me?" Patsy slowly opened the drawer, pulling it out. "That'd be a nice gesture, of course."

The drawer kept going, foot after foot and inside it was filled to the brim with green peanut M&Ms with strawberry licorice and Reese's cups poking out here and there. "Holy pile of a sugar high..." gasped Patsy, as she kept on pulling. She finally stopped and let go, watching the drawer float straight out from the desk.

"Huh, huh?" Lois smiled, nodding at the drawer.

Patsy snorted. "I have to give it to you. That is impressive." Patsy circled the desk, looking at the back. "You're gonna have to show me how you did that."

Lois clapped her hands together. "Does that mean you'll stay?"

Patsy dug out a handful of M&Ms. "The team's back together again." She shrugged as Lois threw her arms around her, squeezing tight. "Hey! I'm fragile. Not so hard."

Lois laughed, squeezing harder. "You're the best fighter I've ever seen, besides myself of course. Best part is people never see us coming."

"Right? Fools." Patsy pulled out a licorice, giggling as the bendable candy stick kept coming.

"Okay, I might have overdone that a little." Lois waved her wand in the air, cutting off the licorice as it trailed along the floor. The two old friends grabbed each other by the shoulders laughing and snorting, doubled over. "Okay, okay." Lois straightened up, fixing her bouffant and wiping her eyes. "We need to be serious. I'm supposed to set a good example. Lacey Trader barely smiled. I'm not sure I ever saw her really laugh in all the years I knew her."

"Well, maybe she should have. I mean, it wouldn't change the outcome, bless her soul of course, but it might have made the ride more fun."

"Damn, when you're right, you're right."

"How about a tour of this place," said Patsy, holding out her bent arm for Lois to wind her arm through. "And tell me what's inside that black purse you're always carrying these days."

"Are you officially on board?"

"I suppose I am. I'll have to tell the general. Not sure how he'll take it."

"Pinky swear," said Lois, as she scooped up the purse by its strap, dangling off her wrist. She held out her pinky for Patsy to wrap her finger around.

"I pinky swear. Okay, now show me. Where we headed to first?"

"Closer than you think," said Lois, with a wink. "Even Earle doesn't know about this one." Lois set the purse down on the desk. "Maybe shut that candy drawer before we go anywhere."

"On it!" Patsy scooped up the long licorice and folded it into the drawer, pushing it back till it was flush with the desk. "Ready, now what?"

Lois grinned, unclasping the purse and tugging at the sides till the opening was wide enough to fit a full grown witch stepping inside. "Shut your pie hole, Patsy and follow me. This is the small stuff," said Lois, climbing up onto the desk, stepping into the purse and starting down the stairs. "The really cool stuff is down below."

"Wowzers. Okay, maybe I could be your wing man." Patsy pulled open the candy drawer at the last minute and scooped out handfuls, pouring the green M&Ms into her pockets. She popped a few into her mouth and put a knee on the desk, pulling herself up and peering down the stairs. Lois looked back in the dim light below and waved. "Hurry up!" she said, descending further.

Patsy chomped down on the M&Ms, stepping over the side of the purse and onto the stairs, her eyes wide with amazement. "Hey, what does this new gig pay? It better be more than the humans were willing to cough up. Does it come with benefits?" Patsy's voice echoed off the walls as her head disappeared below, the purse reshaping itself and snapping shut over her head.

gent Erickson got out of his car and walked down Haskell Street on the East side of Austin till he got to Martin Middle School. The parking lot was full, and everyone was locked safely inside. He kept going and turned on Comal Street, ducking down the alley behind the houses on Holly Street. He came up behind a weathered bungalow with faded green paint and tapped on the door, nervously looking around while chewing his bottom lip.

A bored wizard opened the door and looked Erickson up and down, the corners of his mouth curling into a sneer. "Silver Griffins are really going downhill if you're one of their top agents. You can't even handle meeting a snitch in the middle of the day." He leaned out the door and looked up and down the alley. "Why are you sweating? You walk here?" He shook his head, holding the door. "This is getting better and better."

"My car has a GPS on it, dumbass. Silver Griffins track all their agents."

"Hey! No need for the name calling. The name is Trevor, not dumbass." Trevor cupped his hands around his mouth, lighting a cigarette with one eye squeezed shut. "Only my mom can call me dumbass. It's her pet name for me." Trevor laughed, followed by a cough and a wheeze.

Erickson stepped into the drab kitchen, scrunching his nose at the smell of old grease that was clinging to everything. "Did you arrange the meeting?"

"Of course I did," said Trevor, hooking his thumbs in his front pockets. "Trevor delivers. I have a reputation to maintain. He's waiting for you in the living room."

Erickson eyed him, looking around the kitchen.

"Hey! This is my cousin's place. Don't be looking down on people's domestic situations." Trevor leaned on the counter and quickly pulled his hand away, his skin sticking. "Aw fuck me." He rubbed his hand on his pants, creating a shiny stain.

Erickson watched him, his eyebrows raised, waiting for him to stop.

Trevor looked up annoyed. "Go on in there. You don't need to wait for me. Better hurry. He's a busy man and doesn't really wait for anyone. People usually wait for him. You must have some good shit to even get him to show up at all."

Erickson swallowed hard, his chest tight and walked into the living room.

"I was about to leave." Wolfstan Humphrey looked up with a bored expression. He was sitting in the one decent chair, his hands forming a steeple.

Erickson glanced over his shoulder, chewing his lip again.

"You're already here, dear agent. Let's get this done and you can get what you most desire. Be brave for just five minutes more." Wolfstan watched Erickson come hesitantly into the room, not blinking as he gestured for the young agent to sit down. "Do it," he growled.

Erickson felt a cold chill go down his back as he perched on the edge of a wobbly wooden chair. "How do you know Trevor?"

"Trevor served a little time in Trevilsom. The Silver Griffins picked him up for burglary with the use of a wand. Greedy little fucker. He was stealing entire contents of houses. I'm afraid Trevor isn't big on subtlety."

"Do you have the names and locations of refugees?"

"Very well, then. Straight to business. Enough names to keep you busy for a few solid months of mayhem. Do you have the names and locations of Silver Griffin agents?"

"The entire East Coast. It's all I could get for now." Erickson handed over a small green flash drive.

Wolfstan waved his hand over his own flash drive in the palm of his other hand. "Then we're even. You now have everyone in the Texas area."

"How is that even?" yelped Erickson, jumping to his feet.

"Because I said so..." Wolfstan slowly rose, dropping the flash drive at Erickson's feet. "Next time, be here five minutes early or don't come at all. You know, the reason I waited was because of your mother. Lovely woman. She always gave me extra bread in Trevilsom. This makes us even. Cross me again and there will be consequences. I mean, that's the only way anyone learns, right?" He brushed an unseen piece of lint off his tailored pants. "I understand your kind is hunting a consultant of mine. A wizard from the dark families named Sirius."

Erickson flinched and licked his dry lips. "This isn't part of our deal."

"Everything is negotiable, at least for me. Make sure he stays unharmed and free just a little longer. Then I'll tell you where to find him, myself. You had better get going before the Silver Griffins somehow track you here." He let out a raspy laugh. "Tell me something Erickson. Why would you willingly destroy a very old organization just to get what you want? I mean, I know I'd do it and go get lunch, but you?"

"The Silver Griffins are the ones who get to tell magicals what is justice. If it doesn't fit within their parameters, there's retribution," he said, bitterly.

Wolfstan smiled, pulling out his handkerchief to open the door. "One of the drawbacks of doing business with you. No portals in case the powers that be spot something. You and I are not all that different. But what did all these refugees do to you?"

Erickson was breathing harder, his fist clenched. "Everyone paints the followers like they were all patsies following the charismatic Rhazdon." His eyes shone making Wolfstan smile harder and hesitate at the door.

"Go on. I love a good origin story."

"My grandparents were from Oriceran. Born and raised and planned to always stay. They had eight little witches and wizards, one of them my mother. One day they came through looking for recruits and when my grandparents refused, they burned everything to the ground and put a curse on my grandfather, breaking his magic."

"Ah, revenge. I find it's really hard to focus until that's out of the system. I'm having a little problem like that of my own. I'm hoping your list will help me identify the rodent running loose on my premises."

"The Silver Griffins have gone beyond their usefulness. We need to bring in change by any means necessary."

"You think you're being of service. That's rich." Wolfstan opened the door, a gust of wind blowing in and ruffling Erickson's hair, leaving him feeling cold.

"At least I know I'm being selfish, and I just don't care," said Wolfstan, leaving, the door closing the door behind him.

Erickson wandered back into the kitchen and found Trevor eating a bologna and mayonnaise sandwich, mayonnaise oozing out the sides. "Love these things," he said with a full mouth.

"Forget I was here," said Erickson, laying the envelope with the money on the metal table.

"Already forgotten. Nice doing business with you. Just so you know, fifth time you get a discount," he said as Erickson walked out the back, hurrying along, Trevor's cackle still echoing in his ears.

CHAPTER NINE

Yumfuck headed out of the townhouse by the back door, staying close to the buildings till he got to the neighbors three houses down, slipping under the fence. Marcy was on her back porch shaking out a rug, singing as the troll made his way to the wooden stairs hanging off the back of the building.

He got to Marcy's floor, slipping behind her as she went inside just before the door closed. "I know you're behind me." Marcy turned around, smiling, looking down at the five inch troll. "Out taking a stroll?"

"Looking for company. Leira and Correk are gone most of the time these days..."

"And you're left home alone."

"Only a good idea in the movies." Yumfuck let out a deep sigh, crawling up onto a chair and resting his chin in his hands.

"Hey, that's not like you." Marcy looked at him more closely. "Sometimes I forget how sociable trolls are and how big your clans can get. Alone must be a weird concept.

You need to hear a few stories about this world that I'll bet you don't know."

There was a tap-tap at the door and Portia came in through the living room carrying warm muffins, followed closely by George. "We were overzealous with our baking and have too many. You want a few?"

The troll stood up, reaching his hands in the air.

"Oh Yumfuck, you're here too. Perfect. It's a better day already." Portia held up a muffin, balancing the Tupperware in her other hand. She handed it to him with the paper side and the troll spun it over his head till the warm, sweet muffin was touching the top of his head. A dreamy smile came over his face and he lifted it just high enough to open his mouth wide and bury his face. "Mmmm, blueberry."

"George, tell Yumfuck that story about the mermaids." She nodded to him, giving George a look. "Yumfuck's been hanging out at home alone. He's looking for company."

George's mouth formed into a perfect 'o' and he set himself down in a chair, rubbing his hands together. "That's a good one," he said, looking at the body of a troll topped with a partially eaten muffin stuck on his head. "You think he can hear me inside that thing?"

"I can hear you," squeaked the troll, his cheeks full.

"Some days I'd love to do the same thing, Yumfuck," said George, laughing.

"And if it was pie, he'd try," said Portia, sitting down next to him. She tapped George's knee. "Go on, tell your story. You have a new audience. Tell Yumfuck about the time you met the mermaids from the Atlantic Ocean."

"That is a good one. Let me set the scene for you. The

year was nineteen thirteen and the big war was yet to come. The flu was a winter nuisance. Everything was going great." George squeezed one eye shut, looking up at the ceiling. The troll had eaten his way to the other side of the muffin and was wearing it like a large, crumbly hat.

"George is engaging his brain," said Portia, giving her husband a nudge.

"You know how sometimes things happen to a world and we're all in the same leaky boat together? And then sometimes, something strange happens to one small corner of the world and everywhere else life has gone on without a ripple. This is that kind of story."

Yumfuck let out a belch and turned his head slightly, eating the muffin on the right side of his head, listening raptly.

George furrowed his brow, searching his memories. "I was in Longport, New Jersey, the pearl of Absecon Island. What a beautiful place that was, even in December. The sea would turn foamy and a thousand shades of green." He shook a finger in the troll's direction. "A winter storm, big deal. There were plenty of them in that part of the world."

George tapped the side of his head. "But this time was going to be different. It was just the beginning of something, which none of us knew just yet. Not even the magicals. That's the thing about weather. It can still confound a witch as much as a human. It's what can make a sunrise so wondrous or a storm so threatening."

"Get on with the story, George," said Portia. Marcy smiled and took a seat across the table, grabbing one of the muffins.

"Right, okay," he said, holding up his hands, his bushy

eyebrows dancing up and down. "I worked as a teacher in those days. Taught eighth grade history in those days."

"Perfect job for a magical," said Marcy. "We actually lived a lot of it."

"That's what I was thinking. The first storm came through two days after Christmas, winds tearing off shingles and sweeping away sand. Most of it was to the first ten blocks of the island. We lived on 8th Avenue by an old hotel. At the tip of the island was an old lighthouse that helped ships trying to pass between Ocean City across the bay and the tip of Longport. That end was known as the Point and was shaped like a light bulb."

George shook his head, looking out the window at the clear skies. Yumfuck ate the other side of his muffin hat, his eyes wide as he hung on every word.

Elijah came in the kitchen door and received a loud hush from the troll, swallowing the last of his muffin, licking the crumbs off his chest.

"What's happening? Oh, George is telling his mermaid story. What part is he at?"

"First storm," said Marcy.

"Oooh, it's just getting good. Hey, muffins." He reached across the table and grabbed a muffin, taking a chair behind the troll.

"The storm was a nuisance but nothing we couldn't handle. Life went back to normal. But then a second, a third..." George paused, wiggling his eyebrows as Portia smiled.

"Then there was a fourth storm and the ground was soaked. There was a puddle of water just above the street level that seemed to stay forever. The bulkheads were torn apart, but still we were managing to make do. And given some time everything would have rejuvenated itself."

"But then..." Yumfuck stood up on his tiny legs, clamping his paws on the top of his head.

"But then in July of nineteen-fourteen an unusual summer storm hit the island and pushed at the fragile beaches." George pressed his eyes closed, gently shaking his head. His eyes popped back open, startling Yumfuck who let out a squeak and a fart.

"There were entire houses floating in this cauldron of water. I remember seeing Lincoln Pratt, the fire chief in his second story window, calling out for help. The house was keeling sharply to the right, making the window more of a hatch and the rain was still beating down on our heads the entire time." George swallowed hard as Portia handed him a glass of water and he gulped it down. He put the glass down and waved his hands around. "The noise was unbelievable. It wasn't just the houses that were ripping from their moors but the land itself. Ten entire blocks of land were tearing away from Absecon Island."

"Where were you the whole time?" asked Yumfuck, grasping his hands in front of his tiny chest. "Were there any trolls on the island?"

Portia smiled and gently petted the top of Yumfuck's head, handing him another muffin. "No trolls, dear."

"Well..." George shrugged but Portia arched an eyebrow at him, and he went on with his story. "I was on top of the boarding house where I was staying, holding on for dear life. The entire rooming house was quickly throwing itself out to sea. I was holding on to the peak, lying flat against the shingles trying to ride out the crests that were rising high into the air."

Yumfuck took several small bites of the muffin, squeezing it against his chest like a comforting pillow.

"But on the fourth or fifth crest... I can't be sure. There were so many, and I was getting banged around pretty good. The jig was up. I lost my hold and I got dumped in the drink. Oh two moons, I figured it was over for me. My wand was washed away somewhere, and I was taking in salt water too fast to say any kind of spell, much less think of one big enough to get me out of that mess." He leaned close to the troll. "I mean there was no shoreline to return to. Imagine that!"

Yumfuck squeezed the muffin even harder, pushing it closer to his mouth. He licked the top and leaned back from George, holding his breath.

"My head was pounding, and I had taken in too much sea water when I slipped below the surface and was making my peace with the end. But then..." He paused again, shaking out his arms as the corners of his mouth curled into the beginning of a smile.

"These lovely hands appeared in the dark waters, grabbing me by each arm and pulling me toward the surface. There was so much debris and sand spinning in the water that at first, I had no idea what clever magicals were rescuing my sorry ass. I mean, the waters were too rough for a human being to be swimming out there, but I didn't think even a witch could pull it off and I was right!"

George sat back and slapped his knee, grinning. "My head bobbed above the surface and I spit out just as much water as I took in air, blinking against the waves and the rain and saw that I was surrounded by two mermaids! They were riding the waves just as easy as you and I take a stroll down a flat sidewalk, holding on to me and making sure at least my nose was just above the waters. Then I feel something kind of solid and big move underneath me like I'm sitting down and pushed me up even higher. There I am, moving against the current like some kind of superhero..."

"Aquaman!" squeaked the troll, opening his mouth wide and biting down into the muffin.

"Exactly, just like him. And I'm riding toward 11th Avenue, what's now the beginning of the island. I get to where I can stand up and I can finally see there was a manatee below me. A manatee!" George shook his head. "Manatees in New Jersey. You know, they're magical like trolls. Did you know that? Yeah, it's true. They're called the dogs of the magical underworld. Picture a Pitbull's head and body with two flippers and a fish tail. Just as loyal too. They don't bond, mind you, but you get my point."

Elijah winked at the troll. "This story never gets old. Tell Yumfuck what happened to the lost part of the island. Still blows my mind. I went to Ocean City just to see this part."

"A third of the land that was ripped away," said George in a hushed voice, "resurfaced across the bay in Ocean City, gluing itself to that shoreline." George held up his hands, shaking his voice. "They call it the Garden Section now and it's the nicest part of their city. I tell you, weather is still the baddest mamajamma on either world."

Marcy held up her phone and showed Yumfuck pictures of a manatee and then pictures of Longport from the year before the storms. The troll sat back, holding on to the remains of his muffin, his mouth hanging open and crumbs clinging to the fur on top of his head. "That's a great story."

Portia smiled and winked at George. "One of his best. But that's not the end. Okay dear, time for the big finish."

George leaned forward his hands on his knees. "Years later I wanted to go back and try to find the mermaids who saved my life, but how do you do that? I mean that's a big ocean. They could be anywhere and do mermaids migrate? Do they live near coastlines? I didn't know any of that stuff back then. So, I did the only thing I could think to do and I wrote my story on a note and put it in a bottle and threw it in the ocean." He shrugged, shaking his head.

"Awww that's not a great ending," sighed Yumfuck.

"But wait," said George, pointing a finger in the air. "One day, decades later on a hot August day in Texas an old Light Elf shows up at my door, leaning on a cane. He calls himself the Fixer..."

"Turner Underwood," squealed the troll in delight.

"The very same. He tells me that my presence has been requested in the Atlantic. By then, I've forgotten all about my note and wonder what the hell I've done to bring this down on my head."

"We were married by then and I got to go with George," said Portia, smiling, a twinkle in her eye.

"The Fixer doesn't really give you much of a chance to answer and before you know it, we're in a swirl of magic that's some kind of fancy portal and bing, bang, boom, we're standing on a pretty nice boat in the middle of the Atlantic."

"A yacht, dear. The S.S. Tess and it was a beauty."

"Turner Underwood told me to get in the water and everything would be okay. I mean, at this point I really thought I was a goner. He was a little short on the explanations. Portia was studying him like there was a book written all over his face and she wasn't saying a word."

"I had heard all about the Fixer. He defends, he doesn't attack. Something good was up, I was sure of it."

"And she was right! I got up on the prow and jumped toward the water with a big scream and my eyes shut, but when I hit, I heard a splash but didn't feel the water. I opened my eyes lickety split and saw that I was in a bubble," he whispered. "A bubble!" His voice rose to a shout. "And sure enough the same mermaids came bobbing along, the manatee in tow to say hello. I think it's one of my top ten favorite moments of my long life. I got to tell them thank you and introduce myself the right way. And in return they took me on a short tour of the world under the water. Schools of fish everywhere." George beamed, his eyes shining. "I don't know what I did to deserve such a great life, I tell you."

Portia wrapped her arms around George, kissing him on the cheek. "I think gratitude has a lot to do with it, dear."

The troll lay back in the chair, his cheeks full of muffin, exhausted from the story and content with his company. Marcy went and dug around a kitchen drawer, fishing out a key on a stretchy pink cord. "Here you go," she said to Yumfuck, holding it out for him. "Now, whenever you're lonely you can come on in and make yourself at home."

George dug his key out of his pocket and handed it over too. "Good idea. You can have mine, too."

"I'll get you a key too," said Elijah. "This building is your second home."

"Third," said Yumfuck. "There will always be a home for me in Texas behind a bar on Rainey Street."

Leira chipped away at the old tile floor in the kitchen, the news playing in the background.

Today, what appears to have been an unusual manatee was playing in the Lincoln Memorial Reflecting Pool.

Leira froze, the chisel in mid-air. She slowly turned and looked over her shoulder at the TV and saw the troll in the shape of a manatee splashing in the water, a ridge of green hair along the top of his head.

Authorities were called but by the time they arrived the manatee had mysteriously disappeared, and no one was able to say how it got there or how it was taken away. Another Washington mystery.

Correk walked into the room just as a commercial for Texas Ted's Dealership came on the TV.

"We should keep better track of the troll," said Leira, going back to scraping up a tile. "He is getting into some freaky shit."

"Good luck with that."

Leira looked up and saw the boxes of fun sized Cheetos bags in Correk's arms. "What are you up to?"

"Creating a ward around my new hiding place," he said, wandering back down the hallway.

"I love them, but they are both some fierce kind of weird," said Leira, managing to get up another tile.

CHAPTER TEN

The two witches crested the hill, their wands drawn. The taller one waved her wand, stirring up a small cyclone that took the same shape as the witch and whipping it at their quarry. Sirius spun around like a top, his thick mane of silver hair standing up straight. The arms of the cyclone reached out for him, grabbing him around the waist, drawing him closer.

But the dark wizard still managed to hold up his wand, screaming a spell into the wind. A rip opened up in the earth between Sirius and the Silver Griffin agents, sucking in the cyclone and buying him enough time to get up and keep running.

Louie came up over the hill, running after Sirius, his sword drawn and directing his footsteps. *Move to the East. Hold the sword in two hands, rest it on your right shoulder.*

Behind him, Erickson was catching up, his brows knit together and sweat forming on his lip as he galloped down the hill after everyone else.

"Agent Eighty-Two, keep up," yelled the taller witch.

The other witch looked back momentarily, waving to Erickson. "Come on! You were the one who wanted to be here. You have to earn that medal, Agent Eighty-Two."

Louie was quickly covering ground, moving to the East, staying behind the first line of trees and keeping Sirius in view. The dark wizard was focused on the three agents behind him, throwing fireballs and attempting to open a portal, only to be interrupted by a volley from one of the witches.

The lead witch noticed Louie's position and kept hurling fireballs at Sirius driving him closer to the trees. Too late, Erickson saw where the artifact collector was and calculated where Sirius would meet up with him. He ran at Sirius, his wand extended and waited till the last possible moment, sending out a bolt of lightning that seared Sirius' side but otherwise missed, taking out a large oak tree just ahead of him that was towering over Louie.

Sirius screamed out in pain as Louie jumped back out of the way, losing sight of Sirius. *Traitor*, whispered the sword, and Louie looked up in time to see Sirius open a portal and jump through headfirst, disappearing in a pop of silver sparks. "No kidding," muttered Louie. "Gonna need a little more intel than that, sword." He stepped over the large fallen branches of the tree, frustrated, stomping his way over to the Silver Griffin agents as he strapped the sword to his back.

"We'll get him next time," said Erickson, sweating profusely, darting glances at the two witches.

"Yeah, sure..." said the tall witch, narrowing her gaze at Erickson. "You're usually a better shot than that. You had a clear angle."

"I got him, you saw that."

"Yeah, not enough."

"We found him once, we'll find him again," said Louie. "Little bastard is hated in several magical circles. Someone will give him up. Probably a relative."

"We should have gotten him here."

"Okay, okay," said the other witch. "We all missed him. We'll find him again and remember, it's dead or alive. For Lacey."

"For Lacey," said Erickson, wiping his mouth on his sleeve, still gripping his wand.

"Hey, you said you'd take it easy on me." Louie leaned back just in time to miss the tip of Ava's foot aimed at his head. He took a few steps back, his calf brushing against the couch they had pushed out of the way, knocking him off balance.

"I missed, didn't I?" Ava Hou whipped her long black hair over her shoulder and tapped her staff against the old hardwood floors. She swung the long pole as Louie rolled to the ground, barely missing him again. Her green eyes twinkled with mischief when Louie groaned and got back up on his knees. He shook his head reaching down to rub his bruised elbow.

"It's fun training you. You're a lot more nimble than others I've trained."

"Is this official training?" He arched his back and lifted his chin, stretching out his sore muscles. "That staff has a hard end." Louie grimaced.

Ava laughed. "I would hope so. It's made of wood."

He made a face and hitched a thumb over his shoulder.

"Your dad doesn't know you're up here, much less training me. Maybe we stop with the banging against the floor or he'll be looking for you to come and tell me to cut it out."

Ava snickered and walked over to give him a hand. "You said you wanted to focus on defense." She pulled on his arm, helping him up, a broad smile on her sweaty face.

"Yeah, but I didn't know how good you'd be at it."

"What is it you need to train for again?"

Louie crossed his arms over his chest, trying not to wince. "I didn't and that was part of our deal, remember?"

"Yeah, I can work with that... for now. All right, let's try this again, but this time try to jump over the staff instead of letting it take you down."

"Oh, is *that* what I'm supposed to be doing?" he asked. "And here I thought you came over to beat my ass a little."

"I did, but I figured you might as well learn something in the process."

Ava got into an offensive stance with the staff out in front of her. She began to twirl the simple weapon as the two of them circled each other. Louie crouched as he moved, watching the muscles flexing in her arms and the small twitch in her eyebrow.

Her right arm flexed, and her grip tightened, the twitch appearing for just a moment. Louie readied himself as she swung the staff low and jumped over it, immediately putting his arm up to block her next move.

"Very good." Ava nodded. "How did you do that?"

"You have tells."

She frowned, moving the staff from right to left. "No I don't."

"Then how did I know when you were swinging?"

She narrowed her gaze, moving slowly around him.

Louie grinned but kept his eyes glued on Ava. "I know you're trying to psyche me out. Won't work."

She let out a yelp and swung the staff wide and high. Louie rolled under it and jumped to his feet. Ava spun and swung the staff at about waist-height. He bent back to avoid it, his arms flailing as he lost balance and fell into the small end table. He laughed as he scrambled out of the way, continuing to move.

"Nice recovery."

"I am quick and nimble like a Kilome.. Like a ninja."

"Uh... Yeah, sure." Ava laughed, one eyebrow raised. "I think being mysterious is part of your shtick."

"You mean charm."

Ava gave a quick shake to her head. "No, I got it right the first time."

She picked up the pace, slashing and jabbing, and Louie evaded every single blow. He was breathing heavily, and Ava could see his confidence was growing stronger.

"Hey!" He chuckled and dodged another jab, reaching for a towel off a counter to wipe his face."

"Not so fast. I have no intention of letting you off that easy." She began a kata, yelling as she attacked over and over, pushing him back toward a tall bookcase bracketed to the wall. His face shifted to worry when he felt the shelf at his back. She raised the staff high in the air and roared as she swung it straight for the top of his head, stopping just an inch away.

Louie tensed, his eyes squeezed shut as he waited for the blow. Ava laughed and tapped the staff lightly on his head. Someone pounded on the ceiling below them and Louie put his finger to his lips, smiling.

Ava let out a laugh, covering her mouth with her hand and walked to the refrigerator in the small kitchen area. She reached in and took out two cold bottles of water. Louie nodded his thanks as she tossed one to him and he opened it, taking a big gulp.

Ava pressed the cold bottle to her forehead. "You let your ego get in the way. A certain amount of pride is good. It makes you confident in your movements, but too much makes you sloppy."

He groaned. "I know. I've been told over and over."

Ava's brow furrowed. "

"Someday I'm going to find out who has trained you before me."

Louie took a quick glance toward the closet where the sword rested in its case behind the coats.

"These movements need to become second nature. You have to be able to go on the offense as well or your opponent will wear you out and defeat you. If they're stronger, they can push toward you over and over again. You will need to weaken them, throw them off, to get the upper hand. When they start to tire, that's when they will make a mistake, and then *BAM*--that's when you strike."

"You should be a teacher," Louie sat down on the edge of the couch.

"Nah. I still have a lot to learn, but you don't know as much as I do so it's easy for me to teach you. Besides, ninety percent of my teacher's job is working with young kids who have watched one too many Jackie Chan movies. Their parents bring them to Chinatown for some *authentic* martial arts training, but they usually last one year, if that. It's a phase."

"Don't like the rugrats?"

"Oh, I like them, just not the ones bouncing around kicking people. They're like you but with better coordination."

"So funny I forgot to laugh." Louie rolled his eyes.

"How has everything been going? I mean, obviously not too bad, since you're still alive."

"Always a good place to start." Louie lifted his shirt to wipe his face.

Ava's face warmed at the sight of his muscular abdomen but grew concerned when she saw the black and blue bruise peeking out from the side, winding toward his back.

"That's good." Ava sucked in her bottom lip, rolling the staff in her hand.

"What's wrong?"

"That's a decent looking bruise. You've been in a fight and from the looks of it, a pretty good one." She hesitated, looking him up and down and finally let out a resigned sigh.

"Aw, you worry about me?" Louie teased.

"Not you." She snorted. "Okay, a little for you." She leaned the staff against the wall and came and stood next to him, hooking her pinky finger with his. "Someday you will trust me enough to tell me about your employment." She stopped him before he could say anything. "The truth and all of it. But I can wait. I'm very patient and there's time. There is time, isn't there?"

"Loads of it," he said, leaning in to get a kiss.

Ava put her palm over his face and pushed his head

back, laughing. "Not so fast. I'm not doing one of those secret love story things. First a proper date and my dad knows too."

"I like your dad, but I'm not interested in dating him."

"Ewww, Louie. All right let's practice a little parkour. I'm obsessed with it and if you ever find yourself in a tight corner, knowing parkour may be the thing that gets you out of it. Your ribs up for that?"

Louie shrugged. "I think so?"

"Well, let's get to it, then."

Ava jumped onto the couch, flipping over headfirst and landing easily on a chair, balancing on one foot even as it teetered on three legs. She leapt for the radiator, sailing over the kitchen counter and using the refrigerator door to redirect herself back toward Louie. The young woman didn't waste any time before attacking, aiming an elbow at his head, followed by a roundhouse kick and then another elbow toward the throat. Right, left, right, left--Louie blocked each blow, lowering his hand as she alternated approaches. She didn't slow as she mixed up the movements, kicking one minute and punching the next. He moved with her, blocking everything and keeping his eyes on her muscles.

"Feel the movements," Ava shouted. "Look into my eyes, not at my muscles. You won't always have time to learn someone's tells. That's right, I caught on."

Louie nodded and kept scanning her movements, picking up on small details. She landed a blow to his neck, sending him tumbling back, coughing. He rubbed his throat and jumped back in, locking eyes with her.

"Concentrate. Look for the patterns. You can use this

with anyone, and you'll quickly learn enough about how they fight and start to anticipate moves. The key to winning."

Ava gave Louie a second, standing across the room from him, her hands on her hips. "Some people are technical fighters like me, and others are brute-force fighters. They throw their weight into it. The brute-force fighters tire faster than the technical ones, but they can deal some damaging blows if you aren't paying attention."

Louie shook out his arms, a flash of pain appearing across his face. Ava didn't hesitate and used the furniture in the room to get around behind him and launch off the coffee table into a back flip over Louie's head. He turned just in time to block her forearm from jamming his face and smiled, moving forward to force her to back up. "You are getting better, and with an injury," she said. "Don't bother denying it. But you should get those ribs checked to make sure there's no cracks."

Louie saw her hesitate and forced her into the corner. The sides of Ava's mouth curled up ever so slightly and too late, Louie realized he had played into her hands.

She swept his legs and sent him stumbling backward a few steps. Not done yet, Ava leapt forward and wrapped her arms around his neck, swinging behind him. She pressed her arm into his neck and applied pressure, bringing him down to the floor.

"You got too focused on what I was doing. When you are in a fight, maintain a general idea of where you are."

Louie tried to nod his head and tapped her arm, his face turning red.

"Force the fight in the direction you want it to go, or

you'll end up stumbling around hoping not to trip," said Ava, not letting go. "Small slips can cost you your life."

Louie choked out, "oranges" and patted her arm. She loosened her grip and Louie took a deep breath. Ava smiled as she released him and stood, letting him fall the rest of the way to the floor. She bent over him, her hair cascading around her face. "Oranges is a strange safe word."

"Just you wait. You'll hear it someday above all the noise and know without thinking twice."

"If you say so. You okay?"

Louie lay there for a moment, catching his breath and images of Sirius jumping into a portal flashed in his mind. He pounded the floor next to him in frustration.

"Hey, what's that about?"

"You're right, I need to hone my skills and get better."

"Somehow I don't completely believe you that there's all the time in the world.".

Louie's phone buzzed on the table near him and he reached up, patting around until he found it. He grabbed it and quickly sat up at the sight of Leira's name on the screen.

"Hello, there."

"Hey, you all right? You sound out of breath."

"Yeah, just practicing some moves to keep my ass from dying out there."

"It's a little harder being a warrior than it was a scavenger."

"I prefer collector. What's happened?"

"There's an informant saying he's seen Sirius. I need you

to check it out. I'll pay you the standard fee, just bring me back the information."

"What if it's his head instead?"

"Take your opportunities but be careful. Sirius didn't get to be head of the families without knowing a lot of ancient dark magic. Never underestimate him, especially when cornered."

"Send me the coordinates, and the name of my connection."

"Already done."

Louie hung up the phone and jumped up from the floor, grabbing his water and finishing it off. Ava stuck her hands in her pockets and looked at him curiously.

"Lessons done for today?"

"Yeah, I got a call."

"Is it dangerous?" Ava said, her forehead wrinkling.

"Maybe not."

"Make it back for our date, okay?"

"Don't worry." Louie put his hand on her shoulder and smiled. "You have prepared me well, Master Splinter."

"Oh, great, now I'm an oversized sewer rat hanging with mutant turtles."

"Well..." Louie teased.

"I'm going." She chuckled, shaking her head. "Dad will be looking for me soon, anyway."

"Doesn't he wonder when you come back looking like you've been wrestling?"

"I tell him I went for a run. Not completely a lie." She pointed a finger at Louie. "Text me when you're done saving the world, okay? That way I know whether to turn this apartment back into storage or not."

"I feel the love."

Ava ran back and quickly grabbed Louie on either side of his face, kissing him hard against the lips and just as quickly grabbing her bag and headed out the door, looking back long enough to take a long look.

"Hey... Louie smiled, watching the door shut. He wasted no time, going into the closet and pulling out the case with the sword. "Time to come out and play." He opened the case and pulled out the sword, strapping it to his back. *Relax.*

"Already with the chitchat. I'm doing my best here."

A burst of warm light moved through his back, easing his muscles. Louie worked his shoulders, feeling the ache in his side ease. "Now we're talking." He went and locked the front door, taking one last look around the apartment. Everything was pushed to the walls and papers were scattered on the floor.

"I like it," he said, pulling out his wand. "Time's up, Sirius," he said, opening a portal. "One way or another."

CHAPTER TWELVE

Leira moved to one side so Correk could read the screen. "Looks legit to me," he said.

"Do the Feds send emails?" Leira leaned forward and read the missive again.

"Why wouldn't they?" Correk opened the cabinets searching for a snack. He let out a mumbled harrumph and moved on, opening the refrigerator and standing in front of it, staring at the shelves.

"I don't know. Feds have always called me on the phone or sent representatives in dark glasses to my door. This time they emailed me an invite to show up there in an hour. An hour. That's also not a lot of time. What if I was busy?" Leira glanced back and saw Correk fixated in front of the open refrigerator. "Hey, there's no magic in that fridge. Food will not suddenly materialize."

"I'm hungry but I don't want to have to combine anything to make it into food."

"Spoken like you were born on Earth."

"I miss the food trucks being right down the street."

Leira let out a snort. "This is Washington, DC. You could walk to so many different places. There are even hundreds of different ethnic foods here. It's food orgasma."

"It's not the same," he said, shutting the refrigerator door and rubbing his belly.

"I don't think I ever realized you like routine."

"What? Of course I do, but I can roll with change. Clearly I can. Since I met you that's all it's been."

Leira walked up behind him and hugged Correk around the waist, resting her head on his back. "I tell you what. Walk somewhere today and I'll make sure that there are always taco parts in the fridge from now on."

"Why not just have tacos in there."

"Yumfuck would eat them. If they have to be assembled, you have a shot at getting some of them."

"Good point. He must burn a thousand calories a minute." Correk jerked his head up, his eyes moving back and forth.

"You're doing that thing," said Leira, feeling a surge of magic running through his body. "So hot."

"Very funny. I've got to go, duty calls. I'll pick something up on the road." He lifted one of her arms at his waist and kissed it, turning around to kiss her on the lips and run his hand through her hair. "Go see what the Feds want. Maybe it's good news."

"I doubt that, but I'll go. They play nicer when they think they're getting their way."

"Do you need politicians to play nice?" Correk took a few steps back from Leira and from the kitchen windows, opening a portal in the hallway. He smiled at Leira as he stepped through, already pulling the portal shut behind him. Leira bent down to get a look at the scenery behind him, her brow furrowing. "Hey wait a minute, isn't that...?" But he was already gone, a few sparks skittering across the wooden floor. Leira stood in the empty kitchen, her hands on her hips, wondering if she should try and follow him. "That was the Dark Family estate." She let out a deep breath. "He's the Fixer. If he wanted my help, he'd ask for it." She pursed her lips, still trying to decide. "Nope, I've been asking him all this time to trust me."

There was a loud scraping overhead and Leira thought for a moment about running upstairs.

She stepped into the hallway and leaned against the railing. "Are you building something up there? That would not necessarily be okay."

"Not really," answered the troll.

"Not really? How can you not really be doing something?" Leira arched an eyebrow and tapped her fingers on the wooden banister. She looked at her phone and saw that time was getting away from her. "Keep it within the confines of your room and no flames of any kind are to be used."

"Deal," yelled the troll as several heavy objects hit the floor with a thud.

"I know you're up to something troll." Leira bit her bottom lip. "Don't open anything to other worlds or... universes... or let anyone... or thing into the house."

There was a long pause and she came around and put her foot on the first tread.

The troll ran to the stairs and ducked his head through the spindles. "Not a problem!" He was gone again before Leira could answer.

"Why does he sound out of breath? That troll can lift a table over his head even when he's five inches tall." She glanced at the time again and opened a portal with the coordinates from the email. A paneled room with a long, high dais with a matching wood front, appeared in front of her just as something heavy scraped across the floor above her. "I am so going in his room when I get back," she said, stepping through and closing the portal.

A panel of five Senators sat behind the platform, patiently waiting for Leira to come further into the room.

No one looks startled by a portal opening in front of them. Interesting.

Senator Thatcher sat in the middle and leaned closer to his mic. "Please take a seat at the table, Ms. Berens and we can get started. This shouldn't take long."

Leira brushed her hands against her jeans and made her way to the table, taking an assessment of the three men and two women calmly staring down at her. She gave a nod to Senator Thatcher and sat down on the edge of the seat, resting her arms lightly on the polished table in front of her. *Hagan rule number one. Let them speak first.*

Senator Thatcher cleared his throat as the man next to him pressed his lips together and scowled. *Good. They're getting thrown off.*

"Ms. Berens, we're part of a new committee, a secret one to address the rise in magic in our world."

A Senator on the far left interrupted, spreading his hands out on the table in front of him and leaning into his mic. "We need your help."

"Decorum, Senator Barry," said Senator Thatcher with a slight edge to his normally smooth delivery. He turned his attention back to Leira, a smile on his face that didn't make it to his eyes. "This committee is even unknown to other committees that have been dealing with magic for generations. Each member here sits on one of those committees."

"Ms. Berens doesn't need a civics lesson." The female Senator next to Senator Thatcher arched an eyebrow and sucked in her cheeks slightly, a heavy gold necklace sliding slightly across the front of her pale pink wool dress.

Senator Thatcher blinked his eyes a few times, gathering himself and laced his fingers together in front of his mic. "Very well, Senator Raymond. I will get on with the reason for this particular meeting. You see, Ms. Berens..."

"You can call me Leira."

"Good, well... Leira, I am going to be blunt with you and drop the need for polish or spin. We are all a bit anxious and we know we're at the edge of something. Here is where we learn how to live together peacefully, quietly..."

"Or watch things break down," Senator Raymond interjected. "Much like human beings, not every magical wants to get along."

"Some are criminals mixed with magic," said Senator Barry. The other Senators nodded their heads, everyone looking at Leira.

"And some are monsters," rumbled Senator Thatcher. "They're growing bolder and becoming more dangerous, as you are well aware."

"What is it you want from me?" asked Leira.

"We want to start a pilot program and create a new kind of federal bounty hunter. Someone who has a chance at bringing in a criminal magical without drawing the public's attention."

"But we need the first person we choose to be our best chance at success," said Senator Barry. "Or the entire experiment could fail."

"If it succeeds then we could hire others as well," said Senator Thatcher. "And there would be different levels corresponding to skill. You would be a rare Level Six, going after the worst of the worst."

"The pay would be commensurate with your skill and the danger you would be facing," said Senator Raymond."

"We would need you to start right away and report only to us or to General Anderson. No one else can know. No one."

Leira took in a few measured breaths, letting silence fill the room. She leaned forward a little more and drew in just enough energy to make her eyes glow. "I have a few conditions. They're not negotiable. First one is, I tell my partner. We don't keep secrets like that from each other and the day may come when I need his help. Second one is I have autonomy and immunity. I may have to color outside the lines, and I won't be checking with you first to see if it's okay. Third one, I don't just do work for the Feds." Leira held up her hand as a Senator opened his mouth. "I have my own interests to take care of and that won't change. Next, pay will be immediately after each job as a direct deposit, no delays and a minimum of fifty thousand a job, going up from there. The last one is I'm going to need medical and dental for my household and I want the same lifetime coverage that all of you have." She tilted her head to one side. "Deal?"

Senator Thatcher let out a breath that was more of a shudder and a relieved smile appeared on his face. "You have yourself a deal. Your assignments will still come from General Anderson, for now."

Leira studied their faces, her eyes narrowing. "Something has already happened, that's obvious and it clearly scared all of you. That's saying something because I'm guessing you have each seen your share of weird already." A realization came over Leira and she slowly stood up. "Things are on the edge of being out of control, aren't they? The balance is already off."

"We normally can depend on other, uh... organizations to stand in the gap, but with their recent loss..."

"Lacey Trader's death threw off the balance just enough."

"Magicals are taking advantage of the time it will take the Silver Griffins to regroup and it has shown us that we need a backup plan and we need it now."

"Then I am your new Level Six Bounty Hunter. Let's see where it all goes from here.

CHAPTER THIRTEEN

Correk climbed over the painted wooden fencing that ran around the back acres of the property. Horses were out grazing, swishing their tails and only a few bothered to look up and see who had come through a portal.

He was far enough away from the main compound of the Dark Families to be outside their wards and detection spells. A breeze moved through the grass along the hill and cloud passed across a sky streaked in purple and red. Correk wanted to pause for a moment and take it all in, listening to the sound of tree frogs and nearby tall pine trees creaking in the wind.

Hard to believe so much dark magic sweeps through here. Correk stayed low, moving close toward the main house. He stopped at the edge of the wards and waved his arm, using a spell from one of Turner Underwood's books, creating a gap just big enough for Correk to move through without being detected.

Magic trails left by recent visitors crossed over each

other along the front drive, each one with varying levels of sparkling darkness roiling inside of them.

The distress call had come from a witch inside the main house of the Dark Families. One of the first things Turner had taught him was that the Fixer answered any call, no matter who was doing the calling.

The house was still being repaired from the fire that had eaten up most of the back of the house, including the old library. Tarps still covered part of the roof. He circled his arm over his head, just as Turner had taught him, disappearing and reappearing inside the house in an empty butler's pantry. Correk centered himself and listened for the call again, finding the remnants of it. She was nearby.

Just outside the door a wizard was getting a cup of tea from the kitchen, his nose buried in a book of spells. "Dragons can be calmed with... Interesting. Hmmm, this might work," he muttered.

Correk waited until the wizard went back into the hallway and crept into the kitchen, letting the witch's trail lead him to a door just off the back of the long, narrow room. He spun his hand around the brass knob, turning it without actually touching it and opening the door a crack. Inside were stone steps that lead down into a dark basement.

It didn't take much for the new Fixer to create a sound tunnel and call down the stairs. "Amelia, are you there?"

"Yes... yes, I'm here." Her voice was an echo bouncing off the walls of the magical tunnel, bending around the curves till it reached Correk. "Hurry, there's not a lot of time before I'm missed."

Correk heard the sounds of footsteps and opened the

door wider, sliding inside and pulling the door shut without letting it click.

"Ariana, we can't do away with everyone in the old guard. Some of them will prove to be useful."

He looked through the sliver of an opening and saw two young witches, one of them pulling open a drawer and rifling through a supply of Kind bars. He pressed his hand against his stomach to stop the growling.

"All they've done is show how inept they are and tangle us in skirmishes with others. They're a distraction."

Amelia's voice continued to reverberate up the sound tunnel to Correk. "Are you there? What do I do?" He could hear her footsteps coming up the stairs and held his breath, ready with another spell if he had to defend himself against the two dark witches.

Ariana pushed the drawer shut with a bang. "They're a distraction that will keep trying to regain power."

"Let them try and my pact with the old Fixer will finally be done and I can dispose of Agnes the way I wanted to all along. We have more important negotiations than those old crones. Like what to do with Wolfstan Humphrey."

The voices mingled, arguing with each other as they walked out of the kitchen. Correk hesitated, his ears ringing from the sound of Wolfstan's name. *Singleness of purpose.* Another lesson from Turner.

He shook it off and started quietly down the steps, meeting the young witch around the corner and halfway down the next set of stairs. He shook his head and pointed down, gently nudging her to turn back around, carefully taking the stairs one at a time.

"I just want to get out of here. Get a life, you know?

Maybe a marriage to a decent wizard and a few kids," whispered the witch. She was trembling in her jeans and sneakers and a faded Nickel Back t-shirt as she threw up her hands, putting them on top of her head. "But this family. They're magical mobsters and once you're in, you're in for life. I was born into it. Nobody asked me if this is what I wanted. I didn't get a vote. Not that there's any voting around here."

Correk let the witch talk, using his ability to dip into the stream to check for any magicals nearby.

"Now the thirty-somethings have taken over and they think they're all that, running all over the house, making plans, issuing orders. Ariana is only eight years older than I am," hissed Amelia, her hot breath in Correk's face. "I'm not going to last but if I just pack a bag and leave the family will send their henchmen to drag me right back. Agnes would have never done that you know. Even Sirius would let you leave. But this new regime, they have rules and none of them are very nice."

"Amelia, we need to go. I know it's hard to leave the only thing you've ever known, but if you want out, this is your chance. Do you still want to go?"

Amelia bit the inside of her cheek but nodded her head, wiping away a tear on her face. "Am I in trouble?"

"No, you're not in trouble. You're going to have to be strong, Amelia, if you want to make it out of there. You'll finally get a chance to lose the dark magic and figure out how to work with others."

She sniffed and pushed her damp brown hair off her face. "I can do that." She nodded again, doing her best to convince herself. "I can be brave."

Correk took her arm but she hesitated. "Wait. I can help you, too. There's a rumor that someone wants to kill a Willen over a ring. All of my cousins are laughing about it. They think it's a joke. Willens are always stealing jewelry. But I found a Willen in our back pasture. He had been tortured but he was still alive. He said to tell Correk he never said a word. That's you, right? That's your name?"

Correk grimaced, swallowing hard. "That's me, come on. We have to go."

She reached for her bag, but Correk stopped her with a shake of his head.

"That bag will help them track you. There's something on it, a dark spell," he said, watching the trail of dark sparkles roll and twist around the leather suitcase. "Leave it, leave it all behind and your next stop will help you get started again."

"But my wand. My mother gave me that wand."

"Last time I'm going to ask you, Amelia and then I'm going, one way or the other. Leave it all if you want to come with me. Or you can stay. Your choice." He held out his hand and waited.

"My choice." Amelia looked down at the bag and hesitated, but she put her hand into Correk's and squeezed tight. "I can do this."

He drew her in closer, waving his hand over their heads, the pair reappearing outside the house just inside the wards. Correk turned Amelia so her back was to the house and held her by her shoulders, looking into her eyes. "This is where I'm going to need you to do exactly what I tell you and don't look back. Can you do that Amelia?"

She nodded her head, her eyes wide.

"When I tell you, you are going to run straight ahead as fast as you can and not look back, no matter what you hear behind you. Understand?"

"Understand."

Correk looked over her head and saw the front yard was empty. *Time to go.* "Run!" he yelled, pushing her through the wards and setting off the alarms. A wizard came barreling out the front door, his wand slipping out of his pocket as Correk formed a fireball and threw it at the wizard's knees, knocking him head over heels, his wand flying from his hand.

Others came out, hearing the commotion and started running toward Correk who turned and saw Amelia running, her arms and legs churning and her long hair floating out behind her head. He started running, forming a ball of light in his hands and pulling it open, throwing the ball as hard as he could ahead of Amelia as it opened a portal. A trick only a Fixer would know how to do.

Some of the witches and wizards chasing them stopped where they were to watch a moving portal open as it sailed over Amelia's head before finally locking into place. But others stayed focused on their prey and were closing in on Correk, just as he wrapped his arms around Amelia and pushed them both through the portal, snapping it shut behind them.

Sparks floated down onto Turner's hardwood floors. Correk let go of Amelia and laid on his back looking up at Turner, who stood over them with his bushy eyebrows raised, tapping his cane on the floor.

"I see you made it. Good job. Maybe next time you'll

come in on two feet." The old Fixer turned and went tapping down the hall. "There's a certain kind of dignity that's expected, Correk." He turned back with a wink. "Most of the time."

CHAPTER FOURTEEN

L eira lifted her head up off the couch and checked the time on her phone. It was quarter to seven, and no one was home yet. She sat up and walked barefoot to the kitchen, stubbing her toe on the same piece of broken tile. "Fuck me. That is moving to the top of the to do list."

She opened the refrigerator and stared inside at the pizza box, old lettuce and two lemons. "One of us has to learn to cook. I'll bet Yumfuck could cook." She swung the door shut and went back down the hall, careful to step over the broken tile and was headed up the stairs when the front door opened a few inches.

She looked down and saw the troll strolling in, his fur sticking out in points along the top of his head. He stopped and stared at Leira and she hesitated, staring back at him, waiting for him to say something. Nothing.

"Okay, this is pointless," said Leira, coming back down the stairs. "You're the one being that I think would happily wait me out and say nothing."

"I've beaten Mara and Correk at staring contests. That's how I got Mara's Oriceran cards."

"She gave those to you as a gift."

"Did she?" The troll walked by Leira, glancing up the stairs.

"Wait a minute. You looked a little relieved when you saw me come back down the stairs." Leira followed behind him as he made his way to the kitchen. "You're up to something. I'm gonna figure it out."

"Will you?" The troll hung from the handle on a cabinet, using it to swing himself up toward the counter. He sat down, dangling his legs over the edge.

"You're a tiny little old weird prophet." Leira gave him a crooked smile and leaned on the counter next to him. "Feeling cocky, okay." She leaned over and smelled the top of his head. "Roses. You were at the neighbors and by the size of that belly, they stuffed you like a Thanksgiving turkey. Too bad, I was gonna go out for tacos. Correk mentioned wanting them and now I can't stop thinking about them."

"I could eat." He pressed a paw to the right side of his belly. "Just enough room right there."

The air suddenly grew still, taking on a shimmer. Leira and the troll leaned forward, watching expectantly. A leg came through in mid-air, followed by the rest of Correk's body. He straightened up, brushing off his jacket, his long hair falling around his shoulders.

"Never gets old," said Leira. "New kind of portal?"

"Draws less attention and lets me go more places." He leaned over and kissed Leira. "I never did get a chance to eat."

"Perfect timing. I'm heading out for tacos with the troll. Care to join us?"

"You had me at tacos. I could eat my weight in them right about now."

Leira scooped up the troll and set him in her pocket. He poked out his head and chirped, "I could eat his weight in tacos."

"Not a contest. We can go to Taqueria Habaneros. Norah swore they're the best in town and we can sit outside."

"Norah? There's a Norah?"

"New friend I met at Angel's," said Leira, pushing open the screen door and stepping out into the alley.

"You ever notice we come and go a lot by the back door?" Correk breathed in and out slowly, searching the area for any magicals. A Light Elf was strolling down the next block over and a witch was in a townhouse on the street behind them.

"It helps when there's a small troll in a pocket and your boyfriend likes to check for enemy combatants in the area." Leira wrapped her hand around Correk's arm, leaning her head on his shoulder as they started to walk. "Nice night for walking."

A rat scurried across the alley, ducking behind a row of trash cans. "We should check on the Jersey Willen and the ring," said Correk watching the rat. He rubbed his temples.

"Hey, what's wrong?"

"My last mission came with a warning. I was saving a dark witch from the family compound. She said she found a tortured Willen. Wolfstan is using the dark families to search for the Jersey Willen and the ring."

Leira looked back over her shoulder. "I wonder if there's a way to pass a message from a regular rat to a Willen."

"Of course there's a way," said the troll, poking his head back out. "The city rats are cousins of the Willens."

Leira looked down at the troll and up at Correk. "Both of you are full of mysteries. This is a very interesting world." She went inside and got a piece of paper, writing a quick note. She came back out, folding it into a small square, looking determined.

"What are you doing?" Correk stood on the back porch as she went down the alley, following the noise, tracking the rat.

"Sending a warning to our friend. I want to make sure he knows." Leira picked up the pace, taking on a slow jog, finally cornering the rat by an overflowing trash can. She stopped a few feet from the rat as it stood on its hind legs, squealing at her.

"Chill," she said, holding up her hands. "I know this sounds ridiculous. Or maybe this sounds like gibberish because I'm talking to a rat. I need to get a note to the Jersey Willen. I think you can do it." She crouched down, leaving the piece of folded paper on the ground. "It's very important," she said, emphasizing every word. "Nod once for yes and twice for no. Not gonna do it? Okay. Worth a try." She backed away slowly, leaving the paper and walked down the alley, not looking back.

"What was that about?" asked Correk, as she came back up on the porch.

"A hail Mary or a dumb Dr. Dolittle moment. I can't be sure."

Correk pulled her closer, kissing the top of her head and the troll settled down in her pocket as Leira smiled, looking back again at the light in Angel's upper window.

The humidity was back the next morning hanging over the city. Evan Dunville could feel the damp air as he walked up the wooden platform from the magical express train far below. He was coming back from meeting with dairy farmers in California, trudging up the stairs, trying to resist loosening his red silk tie.

He got to the top just as an older wizard stopped suddenly, stepping back and squashing the toe of his shined, leather Florsheims, scuffing the polish. Evan scowled at the wizard who shrugged and turned, heading back down the stairs muttering to himself.

Evan let out an exasperated sigh and got back in the flow of magicals heading to work, passing through the wall into the Starbucks breathing in the rich aroma of chocolate. He kept moving, glancing at the long line to buy coffee and walked out onto K Street. There he was met with the usual throng of people hurrying to work. He wove in and out of the stream of people, heading toward his nearby office.

The guard at the desk greet him by name as he walked into the lobby and pulled out his ID card to wave at the sensors.

"Evan, you ready for the meeting?"

Evan looked up and saw his main competition for the next promotion. "Joel, I stay ready, so I don't have to get ready," said Evan, smiling broadly showing very even, white teeth.

"You know it wasn't easy getting this meeting with the Senators from the Agriculture Committee in one room. It's a lobbyist's wet dream."

"I know, Joel. I put together the meeting. Come and sit in the back, maybe you'll pick up a few pointers."

"Very funny. I plan to have a front row seat," said Joel, "after I get some coffee."

"They have free trade coffee upstairs."

"I like the stuff from the diner," said Joel, disappearing out the tall glass doors and into the crowd of people outside. Evan chuckled and turned to flash his card to get past the turnstiles just as a man in a long, grey woolen coat pushed past him, banging his hand out of the way.

"Sorry," muttered the man, deftly flashing his card and turning the light to green, pushing through the turnstiles and heading for one of the banks of elevators.

Evan shook his head and looked down at his hand. There was something sticky on the back. "Pretty sure I don't want to know what that is." He pulled out a handkerchief and wiped off his hand as he waved his card and went through, standing at the back of the group waiting for the elevators.

The doors opened and the crowd surged forward, squeezing into the wide space, but there still wasn't enough room for Evan to fit. He finally stepped back and did his best to look gracious as he waved to a few people he recognized. "Next one," someone called out as the doors shut.

Evan gave a good natured laugh and looked down at his iWatch to check the time. A thin ridge of coarse brown hairs was sprouting under the cuff of his shirt where the sticky substance had been. He could feel the blood rushing to his head, partly from panic and partly from the shift that was fighting to take over his body.

His stomach swirled as he tried to slowly back up from the elevators, sweat forming on his forehead.

"Evan, my man. We still have lunch on the books today?"

Evan ignored the man and pushed past him, the muscles in his shoulders beginning to twitch.

"No, no, no," he muttered through clenched teeth. "Not today, not here. I can't...stop it. What the hell is going on?" He flexed his hand, trying to will himself to stay in human form, but it wasn't working.

He shoved his briefcase behind a tall, potted plant along with his wallet. If he couldn't stop it, there was still a chance no one would know it was him. Better for him if someone took it and ran. Credit cards could be replaced. He dashed into the public men's room just off the lobby and stuffed himself into one of the narrow stalls, gripping the toilet paper dispenser, his body drenched in sweat.

"Bad sushi, buddy?" A voice floated over the stall, followed by a cynical laugh as someone peed at one of the urinals.

911. Shifting and can't stop it. Tell the alpha and meet usual spot. Need help. He texted his wife as fast as he could, the bones in his hands already rearranging themselves, making it hard to hold the phone. "Gaaaargh!" The scream erupted out of his body, filling the bathroom and echoing off the walls.

"Geez, dude," said the same voice, his shoes passing by

the stall as he hurriedly left the bathroom. Evan came out of the stall, clenching his teeth in pain from trying to stop the transformation. He locked the door and stripped off his clothes, folding them neatly and hiding them in the ceiling above one of the acoustic tiles, along with his iWatch and ID badge. Any identifying pieces were taken care of and he could give into what was happening.

He had no choice anyway. The shift was coming over him faster and faster, mixed with a feeling of nausea that was new and different and the taste of bitter pennies in his mouth.

Someone pushed on the door to the bathroom, knocking loudly when they found it was locked. Evan responded with a loud growl and the knocking stopped. The bones and muscles in his back shifted, pushing his head out toward the front and hair grew along his back and down his legs. His incisors stretched down, growing into fangs and claws appeared on what were quickly becoming oversized paws.

It wasn't long before the shift was complete, and a full grown werewolf stood in the men's bathroom of a high rise building in downtown Washington DC at the start of what was no longer an ordinary business day.

The wolf tore at the wood veneer on the door, making long scrapes through the soft particle board underneath. It came away in chunks as the animal's frustration grew and he tore a large hole, pushing himself through. The door easily caved outward, collapsing into large pieces as the wolf bound across the marble floor, his large claws clacking against the stone.

A middle aged woman threw her arm against the young

woman next to her, shoving her back as the wolf ran past them, shoving his muscular body against the glass doors and out onto the sidewalk.

People ran screaming, even as some tried to take a picture, only to turn and run as the wolf changed direction. He made his way toward a nearby alley, sliding on a back hip as he took the corner too sharply. The lessons he had learned when he first became a shifter were kicking in and he was following the emergency plan. Get out of sight as quickly as possible and head for the nearest and densest park.

He could hear sirens in the distance and stopped behind a row of townhouses to let out a mournful cry, hoping someone in his pack would hear him. He crossed over a sidewalk, a man dropping his groceries with a gasp, pushing himself against the brick wall as the oversized wolf ran by him. Cars honked and slammed on their brakes, scaring the wolf. He turned and dug his claws into the hood of a Hyundai in a panic, roaring at the driver who crawled into his back seat.

He turned and started running again, the sirens getting closer, down another alley and let out another mournful howl. At the end of the alley a blue Subaru Forester pulled in with its tires screeching and a familiar face piled out of the car. It was Matt Moss, the pack's alpha. He was quickly throwing down the back seats and opening up the hatch, still careful not to make eye contact with the shifter in that form.

The wolf ran to the back of the car and easily jumped inside, turning in a circle and settling down with his head facing toward the back. Matt threw an old beach towel over the wolf, trying to hide the large body of fur and slammed the door shut, racing back to the front and gunning it down the alley. "Your wife called me," he said in a breathless voice. "It's gonna be okay. We'll figure this out." The wolf shifted his body, lying on his side, the car swaying slightly.

Matt made it to the street and saw the cars at an angle, the Hyundai with rips in the metal and he kept going, driving toward 14th Street bridge. "We're headed to our meeting place in Virginia. You'll be able to roam there without any eyes on you. That'll give me some time to figure out what happened," muttered Matt, looking in his rear view mirror at the two yellow eyes glancing back at him.

CHAPTER FIFTEEN

Correk whistled as he flipped a pancake. "I think I like this cooking." He was up early making Yumfuck and Leira breakfast. The coffee was brewing, the bacon was sizzling, and the syrup was on the table. His stomach growled, and he grabbed a piece of bacon and shoved it into his mouth, groaning with delight as he chewed.

"It's not a breakfast taco, but it's not bad." He turned with the full plate of pancakes in his hand and jumped at the sight of Turner standing in the doorway of his kitchen. "Two moons." He swallowed hard, shook his head, and set the plate on the table. He looked at Turner, as he wiped his hands on the apron tied around his waist.

"How do you get past all our wards so easily? I even know your tricks."

"Not all of them, not yet. Talk to me again in another hundred years and we'll see if you've scratched the surface."

"Joining us for breakfast? I can set another plate." Correk opened the cabinet but stopped when he saw the look on Turner's face

"I'm afraid not." Turner tapped his cane on the kitchen floor. "There's been an incident with a shifter. A man named Evan Dunville shifted at his place of work and couldn't stop it. His alpha rescued him but there's a problem. He hasn't been able to shift back."

"I didn't sense any kind of ripple."

Turner shook his head. "Shifters will always be different. No magic trail, no connection to us. I got an old fashioned phone call. You'd better hurry." Turner slipped a small book out of his pocket. "Take this with you and use the spell that's bookmarked. It's a last gift from Rhazdon when she stayed at my house. It should help you heal the wolf. At least help him shift back."

Correk took the book and opened to the page. "Did you tell Lucius?"

"It's not wise to tell Lucius about anything to do with Rhazdon. Ever."

Correk gave a short nod and tucked the book under one arm. He reached over the table and rolled bacon inside two pancakes and wrapped them in a paper towel.

"Leave them. A room full of anxious shifters and bacon. Let's just say there have been incidents. I'll buy you breakfast afterward." Turner took the bundle from him and put it on the kitchen table as a sleepy Yumfuck came into the kitchen rubbing his eyes and sniffing the air. "Ooooooh bacon. Must have bacon."

"Leave some for Leira."

The troll was already pushing a pancake into his mouth. He nodded, spitting out bits of pancake. "On my honor," he said, crossing his heart with a little paw.

Correk arched an eyebrow and took off the apron.

"Don't make a pledge half-heartedly, troll. Not even over food."

"I meant what I said." The troll peeled off the top half of the pancakes and pushed the plate away from himself. "There, those are hers."

"Tell her where I've gone."

Yumfuck held up a little claw. "Done," he said, opening his mouth wide and starting to push in another pancake.

"Here are the coordinates," said Turner, swirling his cane in the air, the longitude and latitude sparkling in the air for a moment before dissipating.

"Got it," Correk replied, opening a portal and stepping out onto a grassy field. "Remember what I said..." The troll gave him a wink, his furry cheeks full, just as the portal closed. The scent of bacon still clung to Correk's clothes. "That should make it easy for every shifter within five miles to find me."

He opened his hand and let a fireball dance in his palm as he moved quickly across the open space toward a field house backed up by dense woods.

The ground shuddered over and over again and Correk stopped moving, turning in a slow circle, waiting for the shifters to come into view. Three shifters came around the field house and bounded across the grass stopping yards from him. Their lips were curled, showing large, sharp fangs and they growled, the largest pawing the ground.

"I'm here to help. I was sent by Turner Underwood. I'm the new Fixer and I hear you have a problem." Correk let the fireball dance in his hand. He kept his breathing slow and steady and made no other threatening moves. The largest wolf pawed at the ground and looked back at the field house. Correk played a hunch and said, "Tell Matt Moss his neighbor is here."

The wolves looked at each other, the largest one flexing the muscles across his back. Correk waited, ready for anything when the wolf slowly dropped his head and stretched out his front paws before standing back up again. The other two stepped back and they turned, trotting back toward the building.

Correk closed his hand, squelching the fireball and let the ashes blow out of his hand as he followed the wolves.

The door to the field house opened and Matt Moss stepped out, the color drained from his face as the three wolves gathered around him, brushing up against him. He reached down and smoothed back the fur on the head of the largest, grey and black wolf, but kept watching Correk draw closer.

"You're a magical. You're *the* magical. The Fixer."

"You're a shifter and an alpha."

"Does Leira know?"

"She's the one who told me. Don't worry, your secrets are safe with us. Is Angel a shifter?"

Matt shook his head. "No, I'm only a shifter because of those fucking dark families."

"You're new to this," said Correk, surprised. "And already an alpha." He took a new measure of his neighbor, realizing he didn't know enough about him.

"I take it you don't work for the NSA."

"No. Being the Fixer is a full time enterprise. You have a problem."

"A very big one. It looks like one of my pack was

poisoned. He's inside. You need to see it. God, I hope you can help."

Correk's brow furrowed and he followed Matt inside to the far end of the long hall where a small group were gathered in a circle, hiding what was in the center. The men stepped back as Matt drew closer, revealing Evan half shifted back, his feet and hands still like paws and his jaw extended. Thick brown fur grew down his back but was absent from his belly.

"He's caught between the two stases and it's torturing him."

Evan writhed from one side to the next, yelling one second and howling the next. A few men turned away, unable to watch.

Correk pushed past them and knelt down next to Evan, away from the powerful jaws. He floated his hands inches away from the man's spine, quietly repeating the ancient spell.

Evan immediately opened his jaws wide and threw up a hot, green liquid, his eyes rolling back into his head. A man stepped forward, ready to stop Correk but Matt put up his hand, scowling at the small crowd. No one else moved.

Correk kept repeating the spell, holding his hands steady as the magic surged through him. Slowly Evan's body twisted back into shape, his jaw coming back into alignment with his human skull and his hands and feet reappearing. At last, what lay on the ground was a naked man, passed out from the exertion.

Matt took a blanket from the table and laid it over his pack member. "We have to find who did this and stop it before anyone gets hurt. Before any humans figure out werewolves are real."

"We'll do it together. I have an idea of who might be behind this. The only person I can think of who may have developed the technology to create a poison like this. Have you ever heard of Wolfstan Humphrey?"

Sirius sat back on the thin mattress. The old motel room was threadbare but clean. Hunted magicals couldn't afford to be too picky. The Silver Griffins had allies everywhere.

Well, he had allies too.

He looked at the pictures on his phone and breathed a sigh of relief. The poison had worked. Score one for his side. "Modern science mixed with magic, who knew? Next stop, the dark bar to pick up a few magicals." He picked up the motel's laminated list of local hot spots and threw it at a rat poking its head out from under the dresser. The rat squealed as it ducked back, and Sirius let out a sinister laugh.

"Next stop, Matthew Moss."

CHAPTER SIXTEEN

Yumfuck waited under the green wooden bench by the stone support where he was hidden from view. A large pack of Twizzlers lay at his feet. It wasn't long before he heard the familiar sharp tap, tap, tap against the sidewalk. The troll came out from under the bench and crawled up the sides, dragging the bag of candy with him. He positioned himself on the seat and turned his face toward the sun as a breeze ruffled his fur.

"Hello!" He called out to his new friend, waiting for the elderly man to find his way to his usual spot.

"I see you made it back here! Well done," said the old man, finding the seat with the back of his leg and sitting down slowly with a grunt and a sigh. "Are you feeling any better today?"

"Today is a good day." The troll bit the top of the plastic, tearing a hole wide enough to slip out a strawberry licorice stick.

"Excellent. Enjoy every minute of it to its fullest." He leaned both hands on the top of his cane. "You know, I realized I never formally introduced myself last time." The man let out a chuckle and gently shook his head. "I had so much fun talking to you that it just slipped my mind." He held his hand out in mid-air, waiting for Yumfuck to shake his hand. "I'm Samuel, Samuel Akins."

Yumfuck looked at the hand and then at his paw. He blew out a slow whistle and instead pulled out a Twizzler stick and put it in Samuel's hand. "I brought something to share with you," chirped the troll.

Samuel chuckled and took the licorice, bringing it up to his nose. "Strawberry, my favorite. And what is your name, little fellow."

"Boy, okay." The troll stood up on the bench and squared his shoulders. "Yumfuck Tiberius Troll." He waited for a surprised reaction, but there was nothing, surprising the troll.

"A troll! I had a feeling." Samuel settled back against the bench. "This is truly my lucky day! You have no idea." He shook his head, his eyes shining.

Yumfuck trilled, sitting back down closer to Samuel, his tiny legs dangling off the bench. "You're not a magical."

"No, I'm one hundred percent human and glad of it. You know why? We're weird and quirky and creative and clever. We possess the ability to rise above our own desires and give to someone else, even when we are hurting. Not only that, when other humans witness the act, they benefit too. Kindness can spread just as easily as an act of hate. I've witnessed both in my day. That's real magic."

"You're not telling me much about how you know trolls."

Samuel bit off a piece of licorice and sat quietly

chewing for a moment. "Well, that story has to do with a great act of hate, followed by one of kindness. I think the year was nineteen seventy-five. I was a young man with something to prove. Back then I worked for the federal government in the Office of Management and Budget as an accountant. I've always loved numbers. Once you understand how they work, magic pops up everywhere. Take the golden spiral..."

"Still heading down alleys, Samuel." The troll carefully folded a piece of licorice and pushed the entire thing into his mouth, stuffing both cheeks. A man walked past with a small dog on a leash, his small, furry dog barking wildly at the troll on the bench. Yumfuck smiled at the man, red licorice bulging out of his mouth as the man startled. He shortened the leash, pulling the dog along behind him.

"It's amazing more people don't realize magic is real. There's stories about it all around us," said Samuel. "Where was I?"

"Back in nineteen seventy-five."

"Right." Samuel poked a finger in the air. "That office, the OMB reports directly to the President of the United States. Of course, I didn't. I was a Grade 103, pretty low on the totem pole. But that changed pretty quickly. The higher ups noticed my talents, especially at finding ways to save without stripping the teeth out of line items. Politicians love that. It wasn't long before I was working on pretty classified material and learning how to keep secrets to myself."

"I'd say you're still doing a pretty good job of that one." The troll laid another licorice stick across Samuel's leg and pulled out another piece for himself. He held it under his nose, curling up his lip and smiling at joggers. "Look, a moustache!" One of the joggers tripped, piling into the other one.

"I'll cut to the chase," said Samuel, picking up the candy and biting off the end. "I was asked to keep an accounting of a project known only to a handful of people. A budget item that didn't appear on any reports that funded research into the study of.... Drum roll." Samuel patted his knees. "Trolls," he said in a hushed voice. "Hundreds of them."

Yumfuck grasped his paws to his chest, a Twizzler squeezed between them. "You knew a lot of trolls!"

Samuel shook his head, scowling. "Not at first. I found out the government was experimenting on you little fellas. They wanted to know how you morph from one thing into another." Samuel smacked his lips, swallowing hard. "It wasn't pretty. I tried to comfort some of them, but it was pointless. Those were days that made it harder to look in the mirror. One day I had enough of it, and I don't know... I try to live by a code, Yumfuck Tiberius Troll. That way when I lay my head down on the pillow at night, I can sleep knowing I contributed to everyone around me, rather than just take."

Yumfuck stood up, leaning forward on his toes. "And what happened? What?"

Samuel let out a resigned sigh. "I set them all free. Every last one of them. It wasn't easy but once I got a few loose from the drips and wires and monitors, nature took over. The trolls could finally grow to eight feet tall and they took to slashing right and left. Alarms went off everywhere and counter measures were taken. They tried spraying a gas into the room, with me in it, but I was the only one affected. Seems they didn't get how much garbage you fellas can absorb." Samuel rubbed his face with his hands. "That's how I lost my sight. Plum passed out at that point and thought I was a goner."

He shrugged, swishing his cane on the ground. "When I came to, I was safely outside the facility and surrounded by an army of trolls. A tall troll with bright red hair on top told me that the battle had raged on around me. Told me! Those dumb federal clucks hadn't even figured out that you guys could talk. What a bunch of mooks. The troll said that I was now bonded with over a hundred trolls! They would always stay nearby, but I gave them permission, then and there to be free and go live their lives. Took some kind of spell that lets them wander without checking in with me. Sometimes I swear I can still feel the connection." Samuel sighed, lifting his chin to the breeze.

"They had already paid enough," he said. "The fellas stayed and protected me till help arrived. It came in the form of magicals who appeared out of nowhere and got me to a hospital. They said they were part of some secret gang. Silver Griffins, I think."

"What happened to the trolls?"

"Once the witches and wizards had me, the trolls shrunk back down to just five inches tall and disappeared forever." Samuel threw up his hands, the cane dangling just above the ground. "I was fired, of course. Best move I ever made. A new regime was elected and there was a decision to leave me alone. There was nothing I could prove anyway. Word went out through the magicals to protect the whereabouts of all trolls on this world. Most went underground. As for me, I started my own little accounting firm and took care of taxes for magicals after that." He slapped his knees. "Turned out to be a pretty nice life. Do you know, you're the first troll I've had the pleasure to talk to since that year."? Samuel bit his lower lip, his brow coming together. "Can you do me a favor?"

Yumfuck wiped his eyes and laid down the Twizzler in his paw. "Anything."

"If you ever see a crowd of trolls again, can you pass the word along that Samuel Akins says hello and remembers them fondly? Tell them all I'm sorry I didn't act faster. I'd change that part if I could. Oh, what's this?"

The troll had stepped over the Twizzlers and placed his little arms against Samuel's waist, leaning his furry head against his stomach. "You and I are best friends, Samuel. Best friends forever. I have a few and you're now on the list too."

Samuel chuckled and held out a hand, finally getting to shake the troll's paw. "That's a deal I can take. And if you ever need my help, Yumfuck Tiberius Troll, you can count on me."

"Ditto," trilled the troll. "And I'll pass the word for you, one way or another."

"Ah, thank you. Then I will sleep even better tonight. This licorice is great. Where'd you get it?"

"I borrowed them from a friend. Don't worry, he won't mind." Yumfuck crawled up onto Samuel's leg and leaned back against him, purring, happily chewing on a strawberry Twizzler.

Yumfuck quietly shut the door to his room and grew to three feet tall, settling himself in the chair behind his desk. He pulled out a piece of paper and a pen, tapping the pen against the wooden desk and biting his lower lip. "Where to start..."

Dear Hagan,

How about the Pug for a new hidey hole? Lots of local brewskies for you and they have rules!

No idiots. No bombs. No shooters. No specials. No politics. Relax. Drink. Be cool. Behave.

Sounds like paradise. Plus, we can get fries.

I've made a few new friends who all love trolls. Who doesn't? They tell great stories and one place knows how to cook and the other knows where to find good donuts. I can't wait for you to visit and when you do, you can have my bed.

Love - your pal,

Yumfuck Tiberius Troll

Yumfuck yawned, stretching his mouth wide and folded the piece of paper, sliding it into an envelope. He licked it and pressed it shut, yawning again. The troll got up and made his way to the large plant and shrunk back down, climbing into the warm dirt and curling up, quickly falling asleep.

CHAPTER SEVENTEEN

Wolfstan opened a portal at the edge of the wards surrounding the dark families' estate. A line of young witches and wizards were waiting to greet him. He stepped through with a wide grin, his arms outstretched. "Well, now this is a welcome." He looked up and down the line, clapping his hands together. "I think I'm going to like this new regime. New blood. Always a good idea, I say."

"Welcome Mr. Humphrey. My name is Ariana and the new head of the families. Take my hand and I'll take you through the wards." Ariana stretched out her hand and Wolfstan bit his lower lip, still smiling and took her hand, squeezing it. They stepped forward together, the air shimmering around them as the wards slid over their bodies. Ariana immediately let go of his hand, watching Wolfstan Humphrey carefully as they proceeded toward the mansion. "I understand you'd like to do business together." Ariana nodded to another witch who walked ahead of them at a fast clip, going inside the house.

"I believe our interests can intersect in several places,"

said Wolfstan. "An alliance could be mutually beneficial as well as profitable."

"An alliance? That would be a few steps up from a business arrangement. The families have never aligned with anyone outside our lines. Not once in thousands of years. Why would we consider changing that pattern for you?"

"Good question. After you." Wolfstan paused at the front door, glancing up at the large wizard guarding the entrance. Ariana passed by him as Wolfstan barked at the guard, baring his teeth, but the guard never flinched. "Not bad. Let me know if you ever need a new job."

Wolfstan followed Ariana into a large foyer and turning into a long hallway. She stopped at a set of tall doors, one partially open. "This time, after you. Welcome to our humble home." She stepped back to give Wolfstan room. He nodded, still smiling broadly, putting on a show of camaraderie and walked into a large study.

Several younger witches and wizards were scattered across the room. All of them were watching Ariana, waiting for a cue. Jackard was draped over an overstuffed chair covered in a heavy brocade doing her best to look bored. Franco was standing with his back to the tall windows, his chin in his hand, scrutinizing Wolfstan.

"I see you've blended the two generations," said Wolfstan, his smile slipping just a little. "Very wise and mature decision."

Ariana grunted, looking at Jackard till she took her leg off the arm of the chair. "Those two have wisely decided to join the new family structure. They serve in an advisory capacity, only," she said in an icy tone.

A witch stepped forward with Ariana's maple wood

wand. Ariana picked it up and held it lightly between two fingers.

"You're a native of Kentucky." Wolfstan glanced back at Ariana, walking around the room and looking at tall painted portraits of past members of the dark families. "The wand," he said, nodding.

"Juliana was my mother. Sirius was her second husband. My father had an untimely end." A general murmur arose among the younger magicals and Jackard smiled, raising her eyebrows. Ariana ignored them all and waved her wand in the air, creating images made of translucent light. "You want an alliance with us, it will come at a price." Ariana waved her wand again and the book in Wolfstan's hands zipped through the air to her. "A price we determine."

Wolfstan shrugged and walked closer to Ariana, facing her. "Of course. Your house, your rules. Tell me what your heart desires."

"Creepy," muttered a young wizard.

Wolfstan's smile dropped for a moment and he turned his cold stare at the young magical, but it did nothing to scare him. He smiled back at Wolfstan, his upper lip curling into a grimace.

"Mr. Humphrey, we have been practicing our family's style of magic for thousands of years, ruling over thousands of witches and wizards. Did you really think even a flunkie..." She paused and glared at the wizard who finally stopped smiling. "A mere child would be scared by a simple stare from a Light Elf? Even one as devious as you?"

The smile returned to Wolfstan's face and he gave a slight bow. "That only proves I'm finally in the right place.

Magicals who know how to keep their attention on what really matters. Power. Loyalty. Rewards. Now, I'll ask again. The most powerful question there is. What do you want?"

"For starters, we have two simple requests. We want an end to Leira Berens. We lived a secluded and happy existence before she found her powers."

"Next?"

"And we want you to break up the Silver Griffins."

Franco leaned forward at the waist, smiling. "You have to admire the size of her balls, right?"

Wolfstan's gaze grew cold. "Those terms are acceptable."

"Really? Just like that," said Ariana, tilting her head to one side, her wand poised in the air. Ariana looked around at the different magicals in the room. "Did you know there are hundreds of us spread out over this country? And all of us, working together couldn't do those two things. The best we've managed to do is raid the Silver Griffin's main headquarters and wound Leira Berens. And you stand there, confident that you, a Light Elf who's a little long in the tooth can take her out. What's different about you that I can't see?"

Wolfstan did his best to hide the anger creeping up his spine. "Dear Ariana, your family is always attacking from the front. No real plan beyond a massive assault. No finesse, no sense of timing or details. Formidable foes require a lot of thoughtfulness and creativity."

"And you possess both of these things?" scoffed Ariana.

"In spades. Neither one will ever see me coming. Oh, they'll think they do, but in the end I'll be triumphant. I've been counted out a few times in the past, but it's always the naysayers who end up wounded... or worse."

"We'll need these things accomplished in the next thirty days." Ariana gave away her nerves with a quick twitch of one eye.

"If we come to a deal, that's not a problem." Wolfstan furrowed his brow. "You knew there would be some counter demands, of course? Your smiling elders seem to have been aware."

Ariana jerked her head toward Jackard who shrugged and put her leg back on the arm of the chair.

Wolfstan paced slowly in front of the different witches and wizards. "I'll keep my demands simple as well. First, I need a dark witch to help me ferret out a problem."

"Not a problem, but I was told you were a master at magic."

Wolfstan's hooded eyes grew cold. "Don't test me. I need the dark witch to play a part and smell out a traitor. There's a magical in my company acting as a spy. So far, they've eluded all my traps."

"Eluded you? Fine, we love a challenge. You can have your witch hunt. What's your other demands?"

"Only one. I want a seat at your table. That's all."

Several of the magicals gasped and Franco let out a short laugh, his hands on his hips.

Ariana swallowed hard, unwilling to back down. "Bring me Leira Berens' dead body and destroy the Silver Griffins and I'll pull up the chair myself."

Wolfstan stopped pacing and held out his arms. "Then we have a deal. Stop fretting, Ariana. We will raise dark magic to levels it hasn't seen in quite some time and you, young witch will be at the front. It'll be amazing to watch."

"That's one way to put it," said Jackard, nodding to Wolfstan.

Erickson's mouth was dry. He sat in front of the computer in his small apartment staring at the list of names he had gotten from Wolfstan. He had traded his family's loyalty to the Silver Griffins to get it. "It was necessary," he said, looking out the nearby window, swallowing hard.

An anger burned inside of him, rising up when he looked at all the names. "Traitors," he whispered. He ran his finger over the one address he'd been able to find so far. He had tracked a group of five refugees to one street in Belle Haven, Virginia on the Eastern Shore. They were clustered together in a row of houses that lined up opposite the Idle Hour Theatre and were hiding in plain sight in the small town.

"Whew. Now or never." He wiped his palms on his slacks and stood up, his stomach roiling. All it took was a wave of the wand and the portal opened to the coordinates. The Silver Griffin's agent stepped into rural Virginia. He was behind Phillips Hardware, a standalone concrete building that did triple duty as a gas station and convenience store. The smell of fish and salt water was clinging to everything.

Sea gulls were picking through the trash.

Erickson immediately regretted his haste and not

changing out of his suit. He walked around to the front of the store to get his bearings.

Two local farmers passed by him in a truck, giving him a long, blank stare, letting him know he wasn't exactly welcomed.

"You come into town looking like that and you're here to either collect something that somebody still wants, or arrest someone who didn't want to be found." Erickson looked back at the old man sitting in a faded wooden rocker in front of the store. He smiled at Erickson, showing several gaps in his front teeth.

Erickson rolled his eyes and set off down the road. "Wrong on both counts," he muttered.

A boy with bright red hair rolled past him on an old purple Schwinn bike, suddenly speeding up, pumping his legs and taking the next curve at an angle.

"Shit. A lookout. I might as well have worn a fucking neon sign." Erickson took off at a run, his tie flying over his shoulder, flapping against his back. He came around the corner just as the last few people were huddling near an open portal. He clenched his teeth and roared in anger, barreling toward them. He threw himself forward as the last refugee, a middle aged Elf stepped into the portal and looked back at him, wide-eyed with fear.

Erickson was able to make contact with the portal, hoping to read the coordinates. A simple trick, especially for a Silver Griffin agent. But sparks popped and sizzled against his skin making him recoil. Blisters formed along his palm. "What the fuck was that?" He rolled on the ground in pain, dirt and leaves clinging to his suit.

A blue Chevy truck came around the corner and the

driver slowed down next to him, putting down the window. "You having a bad day there, son?"

Erickson laid back against the ground, holding his hand in the air.

"There's a nice bench about a block away if you need some place to set yourself down for a piece. You think you can make it that far?" The older man started to get out of his truck, opening the door with a loud creak. Erickson pressed his eyes shut in frustration and rolled over, bringing himself up to his knees. "I've got this," he spit out, pushing off with his good hand, the other cradled close to his body.

"Well, you've got something. Think about that bench. If the Sheriff drives by and sees you lying prone, he'll provide you with a nice cot to sleep it off. Up to you." The window zipped back up and the truck pulled away, the tires crunching gravel. Erickson brushed off his knees, grumbling and shook his head. A headache was setting in from the hard bounce against the portal. Someone powerful had made sure he couldn't detect a thing.

Turner Underwood came marching down the hallway of his Washington estate, his cane tapping rhythmically. He was dressed to go out but turned around when he sensed the incoming guests. He had seen the tatters of someone else's magic that had accompanied them and saw something familiar. Something that made their hasty exit even more dire.

He opened the door at the far end of the hall, passing

through to the streets of New York City of a hundred years ago.

"Where are they?" he shouted, waving his cane. "Take me to them!"

The magicals out walking on the street looked surprised, glancing at each other.

"Yes, yes, I already can tell where they are." Turner waved his hand, patting his chest. The anger was already subsiding. He hurried down 2nd Avenue to Clifton, shaking his head and muttering to himself. Two witches taking a stroll crossed to the other side of the street, picking up their pace.

He finally got to the townhouse where their jumbled magic was radiating, telling him most of the story. He marched up the stairs, defying his age and pushed open the heavy front door. There in the drawing room on the right were five refugees all huddled together.

Turner stopped in the doorway, pursing his lips to give himself a moment to think. "Well, I suppose everyone is getting hungry by now. I assume Susie is getting you settled?" He forced himself to speak in calm, measured tones. "Good," he said, nodding. "You must all be my guests tonight at my townhouse," he said, scanning the room. "You, can I speak to you?" He gestured to the middle-aged Elf.

The Light Elf pointed to himself and hesitated. Turner nodded gravely. "Come, come, just a few words." He put his arm around the Light Elf as he drew closer, ducking his head down. "Did you get a good look at who was chasing you?"

"No...no," stuttered the Elf. "A man with dark hair. A wizard I think but I'm not sure. It all happened so fast."

"Understandable. You're safe now. Unquestionably safe. Magic can't penetrate this world. No one will ever figure out you're here."

The Elf let out a sigh. "That's good news, of course. But we want to be out there. To be free to choose. Can you help with that?"

"I intend to, sir. Trust me, I will make sure of that too."

Turner waved to the group, giving them his best genial style as he turned and marched back out of the house. He was gripping his cane tightly, making himself walk more calmly. "There's a snake in the garden," he muttered, swirling his cane in a small, neat circle to see the traces of magic again. "A traitor in the Silver Griffins. I'll find you and when I do, I'll put an end to this nonsense. Permanently. In Lacey Trader's name."

CHAPTER EIGHTEEN

Louie leaned back against the wall, looking around the long, narrow bar. The place was dark, from the black paint on the walls to the hanging pictures of wizards and witches from the past.

The old family establishment was situated in DC and was known to be owned by one particular family--a dark one. The doors were charmed to keep the non-magical from wanting to enter. Just in case, the door was painted in gold letters with *Big Al's Pest Solutions* and a cartoon roach running away.

"Geez, you think you could have picked a gloomier place?" Ronnie guzzled his beer and pushed the glass back toward Louie with two stubby fingers. "More, please."

"It's got a certain vibe." Louie lifted two fingers, getting the bartender's attention.

"Yeah, a dark one. Those are some evil wizards they are worshiping on those walls."

"I think they prefer misunderstood. It's your first trip to

this world. I wanted to give you a place to land that felt like home."

Louie ran his hand over the top of the table. "Look at this baby. Carved from Oriceran trees. That is badass. To get it all the way here..." The twisted knotty wood curved around the live edges of the furniture.

"I recognize the name of the family that owns this place. Morgan. They have a reputation on Oriceran too. That is some dark shit."

"We earn a living at the Dark Market. These are our people. Once you come through those old glass front doors, you're in a magical world that's tucked away in the busy streets of the nation's Capital. This is a great launching pad for your visit."

"You're a great tour guide, okay?" Ronnie chuckled, glancing around at the patrons. A wizard with grey hair slicked back close to his scalp curled his lip and snarled at Ronnie. But the old gnome just rolled his eyes and barked loudly, clacking his teeth together.

Louie let out a guffaw but kept one hand on his wand, just in case. The old wizard wrinkled his nose and turned back toward his companions, whispering to them.

"I have missed you," Louie said with a contented sigh.

The bartender strode over, the long-crooked snout marking him as a male dryad despite his attempt at a glamour. He stopped in front of Louie and snarled, wiping off the table and putting down two more beers. "Thank you as always, Norman."

Ronnie watched him walk away, puzzled. "Is that his glamour? What does he look like without it?"

"No one knows but there's a pool going with ideas. I'm down for old, knotted tree."

"Good one. Makes me look like a fucking centerfold." Ronnie lifted his glass, finishing it off in one neat guzzle.

A young, pretty witch in a black sweater and black pants sat down in the chair next to Louie, pulling it closer.

"Little on the nose with the outfit, Freda." Louie glanced at her, taking a long sip of his beer. Ronnie arched a brow and watched, waiting to see what was going to happen next.

"Friend of yours?"

"Of sorts," said Freda, taking a sip from Louie's beer. "We're distant, distant cousins."

"We're not related," said Louie, shaking his head.

"Come on, are you trying to act like you don't know me? I'm fun to have around. Ask anyone."

"You're known to drink a little too much, flash your dark, dark eyes, and not worry what comes out of your mouth."

"It's part of my charm... and just an act. I assume that's why you asked to meet me."

"You said you picked this spot for me!" Ronnie's mouth hung open in surprise.

Freda smiled, running a dark red fingernail across the back of Ronnie's hand. "Oh honey, Louie is always working the angles. Anyone who's been around him for an hour figures that out."

Louie waved to Norman, this time with three fingers.

"That's so nice," she gushed. "Are you buying me a beer?" She shrugged a shoulder, smiling at Ronnie. "You'd think he was hoping I'd let go of a family secret or two."

That's the idea. "No, of course not." He laughed. "Just enjoying having some drinks with an intelligent woman."

"Aw geez, the shit is piling up in here." Ronnie scowled, barking at the table of wizards again. They were shaking their heads at Louie and Freda.

Freda drummed her nails on the table, whispering a spell. The chairs dissolved into ash underneath the wizards, dropping them hard to the floor. The rest of the bar erupted into laughter and pointing as the wizards picked themselves off the floor. The wizard with slicked-back hair stood up with his wand already aimed at Freda.

She pulled out her wand displaying her family's coat of arms down the side.

"Brandeis," spit out the wizard, the color draining from his face. He lowered his wand, gripping it so tight his knuckles were white.

Freda held out her hands, nodding toward the others in the bar. "Take your pick. I won't tell."

"Damn, Freda. Can we ever have a regular meeting without you inciting a riot?" Louie slowly rose, holding onto his wand but keeping it at his side. "A little exchange where nobody even notices us."

Freda's brow furrowed, a sly smile spreading. "What's the point in that? I could send you an email if that's all you wanted." She tilted her head to the side. "You like this as much as I do." The witch suddenly jerked her head to the left, flicking her wand at a Light Elf in the middle of creating a fireball. The fireball turned to ash and the man's hands flew up in the air. "Now, now. We don't need to wreck the place." She whispered another spell under her breath, waving her wand. A wind picked up inside the bar, blowing her hair in a spiral above her head and spreading outward. It settled over the ashes picking them up and reshaping them back into chairs.

"There, all better. Everyone can relax. Next round is on me." Freda's eyes grew cold and she waited for a moment as everyone slowly sat down again, turning away. The wizard hesitated, lifting his wand for a moment but a slight jerk of Freda's chin and he dropped his hand, sitting down.

Freda smiled, pleased and sat back down putting away her wand. "A drink and a show. You're welcome." She licked her bright red lips. "Now, where were we?"

Norman dropped off more beer to their table. Freda pushed the first beer toward Ronnie who shrugged and picked it up, taking a long sip. "She's not all bad."

"Ronnie it should take more than a cold beer to buy your loyalty," said Louie.

"I enjoy my life. Very simple."

"Louie," said Freda, "you came here for intel on the new regime in charge of the families." Freda swirled a finger in her beer, turning the liquid a bubbling black. "Tough crowd. Mix that with their inexperience at leading or dealing with others and it gets dicey. They're unpredictable and out to prove something."

"They're your age."

Freda put a hand coyly on her chest. "I come from a family that believes in training their young from when they're small," she said, holding her hand at table height. "Extensive training in all aspects. But we don't like to get involved with the Dark Families union. Too much infighting."

"Ah, that explains a lot," said Ronnie. "You two do have a

few things in common. She knows your background." Ronnie arched an eyebrow, raising his glass. "You two are more than cousins if he told you about his mother."

Louie's cheek twitched with momentary anger. Ronnie saw it but didn't move. He was used to the reaction every time the topic came up. "Does Leira know your mother practiced the dark arts on Oriceran?"

Louie scowled and said quietly. "Not unless Jackson told her."

Ronnie sat back in his chair. "That's a no. Jackson would never betray a confidence. Not even for his daughter."

Freda's eyes widened. "Leira Berens is Jackson's daughter?" She shook her head. "Two worlds and everything manages to intersect. There's still a bounty on Leira's head. Fools. She strikes me as very pragmatic. If they bothered to trade with her, I'll bet she'd play with them."

"You're not wrong," said Louie, taking a long sip, the cold beer sliding down his throat. "But that's not really news, Freda."

"No, it's not. But this is. The newbies have made a new alliance with someone that does have everything they lack and in spades. I think you know the beast. Wolfstan Humphrey. He's taken on the job for them."

Ronnie put his glass down slowly, his mouth making a perfect 'o'. Louie felt a cold chill down his back, staring at the pattern of the wood in the table.

"This is bad," he muttered, looking up. "What does he get in return?"

"A seat at their governing table," said Freda, wrinkling her forehead. "That's how bad a hard on they have to kill your boss. Watch your back, Louie. The game has taken a wicked turn." Freda got up to go. "One more odd piece of news. There's a rumor that Wolfstan has a bounty on a family of Willens, of all things. They have a prize he wants but they've all disappeared. Something about a ring. He's offering a small fortune to find them. Lots of shiny objects if just one Willen will give them up. I hear he's getting nowhere. Have to give it to those giant rats. They won't turn on each other."

Louie quietly sipped his beer, not saying anything.

"So that does mean something to you. Interesting. Well, I've helped all I can for now. If I hear anything else, I'll be in touch."

"Why are you helping?" asked Ronnie. "No, really, why? Aren't you closer to the dark families?"

Freda let out an exasperated sigh. "Why do you always leave the family tree to me, Louie? My mother on Earth was his mother's twin, separated at birth."

Ronnie's eyes widened. "I thought you said distant cousin."

"Family joke," said Freda, her smile slipping. "One stayed on Oriceran, the other was taken to this world. Family loyalty runs deep, my little Gnome friend. Anyone touch one of mine, I will cut down two of theirs." Freda got up to go, leaning her hands on the table. "I meant what I said. Be careful. That Humphrey is into some very bad magic, even by our standards. The young ones have no idea, but they just signed a deal with the devil and the devil always insists that you pay. Doesn't matter to him if you get what was promised, but you always have to pay."

They watched her walk out, giving a salute to the wizards who barely looked in her direction.

"You were right. This was an interesting start to my vacation," said Ronnie. "What's next on the itinerary? A shifter brawl? Maybe some Kilomeas can track us."

"No, Lincoln Memorial. Or what we call it on Oriceran, Ode to a Light Elf."

Louie pulled Ronnie up the stairs, away from the fetching female Gnome walking down toward the bright red train below. Ronnie pulled his arm away and leaned over the side. "What's your number?" he yelled to her.

The Gnome flicked her long blonde hair and looked back at Ronnie with a smile and a wink before she blended back in with the crowd pushing to get down to the train before it left.

"Let's get going, lover boy," said Louie, shaking his head. He tugged on Ronnie's arm again just as the crowd pushed behind him, forcing him toward the top of the stairs. "Oof! Hey, no touching the bits!" Ronnie was jostled to and fro, frowning and doing his best to stick out his elbows.

Louie pulled him out of the stream and marched him through the wall into the Starbucks at E Street. Ronnie sniffed the air, his shoulders relaxing. "Chocolate," he muttered in surprise. "Nice."

They made their way past the tables already filled with writers tapping away on laptops with cold coffee next to them. "Is that some kind of job on this planet?"

"You'd think so," said Louie.

Ronnie look surprised, his head on a swivel, taking in every detail.

They came out onto the wide boulevard filled with tourists and people trying to get back to work. The humid air hit Ronnie in the face, lingering till fall would finally arrive.

"This way," said Louie. "We have a hike in front of us but there's plenty to look at on the way."

"Yeah, all these people and those... those..." Ronnie pointed at the cars zipping down the road, gliding in and out to get ahead of each other. "It's like there in a race with each other."

"Yeah, I thought the same thing the first time I saw it."

"Louie! What are you doing here?" Ava stood in the middle of the sidewalk, her arms loaded down with bags.

Louie startled, the blood draining from his face and a ringing starting in his ears. He stammered, his mouth opening and closing without a word coming out. Ronnie rolled his eyes and put out his leathery hand, smiling a toothy grin at Ava. "Hello, I'm Ronnie. This one's best friend. I take it you two know each other?"

Ava giggled, jostling the bags in her arms, peeking between two of them. "He rents an apartment from my father." She smiled, dimples appearing in her cheeks. "We own the restaurant below his place."

Louie's face reddened and he swallowed, trying again to say something. "You look great."

Ronnie smiled, his forehead wrinkling.

Ava giggled again. "Thank you? Where are you two headed?"

"Louie's showing me around town. This is my first trip to... to Washington."

"Oh, you picked a great time to visit. Make sure he takes you to the Air and Space Museum. That one's my favorite." The packages slipped in her arms and Louie caught them from the bottom, helping her rebalance everything. His face came close to hers and he could smell her perfume. He looked in her eyes and stopped moving, frozen right there.

Ava leaned forward and kissed him lightly on the lips. "I have to get going. I have the dinner shift and this stuff is getting heavy."

"Yeah, sure. That's a good idea," said Louie, the ringing back in his ears.

"Nice meeting you," said Ronnie, glancing at his friend and shaking his head.

Ava smiled and turned, quickly making her way down the sidewalk, turning the corner.

Ronnie elbowed Louie, an eyebrow arched. "I've never seen you like this. You have it bad."

Louie came to and realized his mouth was dry, but his palms were sweating. "Yeah, I think I do. That could be trouble."

"Good trouble, my friend. And finally. This world may be good for you." He slung his arm as high as he could around his friend's shoulders. "We're off to see the wizard."

"Love that movie," said Louie as they began to walk down E Street.

"The best. My people have never looked so good."

CHAPTER NINETEEN

Wolfstan came late to his own dinner. He wanted to make an entrance into the back room of the Capital Grille. The room was dark paneling with blood red walls and old paintings in gold leaf frames. A long table was set up down one side of the room with a large model sailboat at the far end behind where Wolfstan would be sitting.

The group of eleven Senators he had managed to gather looked up from their tight clusters around the room. They were all seasoned practitioners of an engaged blank face and waited to see what was going to happen next. A few swirled the whiskey in their glasses, the ice cubes making a loud *clink* in the suddenly quiet room.

Several had brought aides with them who stood by the elbows of the more powerful Senators. They would be fed later in the kitchen at a card table with cold sandwiches and a soda.

"Welcome!" Wolfstan's voice was cheery, booming over their heads with his arms outstretched. The young Senator from Michigan smiled broadly, taking a swallow of his whiskey.

"Pace yourself, young man," said Senator Bleeden. "There'll be an entire night of ass kissing. Don't want to get started too early."

Wolfstan made his way through the room, smiling and shaking hands. A waiter delivered a glass with two fingers of Ranger Creek bourbon in a crystal glass. Wolfstan took the highball from the silver tray, swirling the contents without taking a sip.

"I see the show has already begun. Didn't know the restaurant had silver trays," muttered Senator Thatcher. He watched Wolfstan carefully, a look of slow boredom on his wrinkled face, learned over decades of attending Senate hearings. Wolfstan raised his glass to him, acknowledging his seniority in the room and Senator Thatcher returned the gesture. His aide stood quietly at his elbow, his hands grasped behind his back.

"Thank you for accepting my invitation to dine with me tonight." He unfurled his fingers, blowing into his palm for dramatic effect. Glowing blue and green stars floated up to the ceiling as the lights dimmed, bathing the room in a soothing glow. A few of the Senators looked up, their mouths open and a murmur grew in the room. "Dining by starlight without having to go outdoors," said Wolfstan, smiling.

Senator Thatcher let out an exasperated sigh and sipped his drink, never taking his eyes off Wolfstan Humphrey.

"I want to propose something. A merger of sorts," said Wolfstan, looking around the room.

"You didn't need an entire dinner to ask for an agreement with an Oriceran company," said Senator Bleeden. "We've already established ties."

"True," said Wolfstan, his eyes growing cold. "But where has it gotten you? I mean, *really* gotten you. I understand Charles Monaghan has disappeared on you and the multinational agreements he made are fraying at the edges. And you have no representative watching over anything on the other world. Obvious holes that could turn into big problems."

"You said merger, not agreement. What are you proposing?" Senator Thatcher's voice was approaching a low growl.

Wolfstan let out a sigh, tapping his chest. "You need someone to advise you. Someone who has interests on both worlds to give you insight on a regular basis."

"That would be a conflict of interest. We can't agree to do business with you and then let you also call the shots."

The other Senators watched the pair volley back and forth.

"Absolutely. It wouldn't be... fair. Fleeker is a separate issue and has no contracts with the government. No conflict of interest. Let's keep it that way. Instead, I'm offering my services, behind the scenes of course."

"Of course." Senator Thatcher swallowed the rest of his drink and handed the glass to his aide.

"I can advise you on magical issues and help ward off pests before they become problems."

The young Senator's face brightened. "Like Leira..." Senator Thatcher cut him off with an icy look. He crossed his arms over his chest. "Let's make this easy on both of us.

Why don't you come up with a formal proposal and send it over to my office? My aide will ensure it's distributed properly. That way we can enjoy our dinner without getting in the weeds of the details."

The broad grin was fading from Wolfstan's face. "Of course. There's time to discuss how it can be mutually beneficial. Let's use tonight to get to know each other better. It's always easier doing business with a friend." Wolfstan nodded to the restaurant's manager and the Senator's made their way to the table, picking chairs according to their ranking in the room. Wolfstan sat at one end and Senator Thatcher chose the other, leaning toward his aide at the last minute. "Make a note to remove the fine Senator from Michigan from any confidential magical briefings. See that he gets something that will keep him happy but cut him out of the loop."

The handful of other aides were making their way toward the door. Senator Bleeden's aide brushed past Wolfstan, his hand glowing for a moment as he passed a thumb drive and followed the others out of the room.

Senator Thatcher took his seat, pressing his lips together, his hands resting on the table. He had seen the glimpse of purple light but was too smart to say anything. There was a traitor working for them, a dangerous magical turncoat. "These are very dangerous times," he said, looking at Wolfstan.

"Indeed," replied the host. "You can't be too careful if you want to make it through safely. May take a magical guide to get to the other shore."

"We shall see." *And it will be Leira Berens.*

CHAPTER TWENTY

Leira tapped on Yumfuck's bedroom door and the small troll opened it a crack looking up at her. "Yeah?"

"What do you mean, yeah?" She tried to look into the room, but the troll noticed and pulled the door shut a little bit more.

"Can I help you?"

Leira narrowed her eyes, her hands on her hips. "I sometimes lie awake at night wondering what you're building in here."

"A little privacy goes a long way."

Leira stared at him for a moment but Yumfuck didn't blink. "Fine. For now. I came up here because I have a request that came my way and your unique skills are required."

"Hang on." Yumfuck abruptly shut the door and Leira could hear something heavy sliding a short ways across the floor. "What are you doing in there?" She tapped on the door again.

The troll opened the door, sliding out and pulling the door shut behind him. He was wearing his blue mask and cape and positioned himself in front of the door, his hands on his hips. "I'm ready."

"I'm not sure all this was required. Never mind, I get it. You're Batfuck." She leaned down and held out her hand, scooping him up and putting the tiny crime fighter on her shoulder. "There's been reports of a strange bear loose in Fort Dupont Park." Leira pulled out her phone and held it up where Yumfuck could see the blurry photos. "Look familiar?"

Yumfuck gasped, his little paws on his knees. "Troll!"

"That's what I thought too. But he doesn't look quite right. His fur is matted and full of burrs."

Yumfuck let out a mournful cry, leaning his head back and yowling. Leira scooped him off her shoulder and held him up where she could see him. He looked pained and the tips of his fur were turning a deep navy blue.

"OOOOWWWOOOOOOOOO!"

"Whoa, little buddy. Hey there." His mask was askew and Leira carefully took it off. She stroked his fur pulling him close to her cheek. "You're okay. I'm here." Leira looked at the picture on her phone. "Yumfuck, tell me what you saw."

"OOOOOOOOOOOO!" The mournful cries continued and Leira could feel shudders passing through his little body. She held him up where he could see her face. "Yumfuck," she said sternly, getting his attention. "Tell me. We're a team. Let me help."

The troll brushed a paw against his wet eyes, matting his fur. "That troll has lost his person. The bond was severed. He's lost his way," cried Yumfuck, letting out another baleful howl. "YOOOOWOOOOOOOO!"

Leira ducked her chin in surprise. "Fuck me. I didn't know that was possible. I thought if I died... well, you know. You go too."

"There's one way and only one way. Before the magical died they must have severed the connection with the spell."

"*The* spell. There's a spell. You never mentioned that there's a spell. Correk never told me there's a spell."

"Trolls would rather die than have the bond ripped apart. That's what the spell does. It rips it apart. Part of the troll still dies with the host."

"Damn that's harsh."

"Most trolls lose their minds when that happens. They lose their purpose, their ability to think clearly. YOWOOOOOOOOOO!" He leaned his little head back, the cape draping around him.

"A magical died near here. Yumfuck I need you to focus. Can you tell how long the troll has been wandering in the park? Come on little guy. Little motherfucker take a look at the picture. Be the superhero I know you can be. Be Batfuck and tell me what you see. Maybe we can help."

Yumfuck let out a last shudder and wiped his face again. He threw back his shoulders and straightened his cape. "Let me see the picture," he said, resolutely.

"That's the way we do it." Leira held up her phone. "The smallest detail can help."

"Look at his eyes. They're growing cloudy. I'd say he's been running loose for maybe a month. It's only going to get worse for him till he can't really see clearly and then he becomes dangerous."

"Then we need to go find him now. I'm proud of you little buddy." She put him back on her shoulder and opened a portal in a dense part of the three hundred and seventy-six acre park. Leira stepped through, closing the portal behind her. She pulled in magic through her feet, her eyes glowing. "Any thoughts on how to help the troll?"

"There's only one way. He has to find a new magical and form a new bond."

Leira looked at the trail of magic along the ground. "Just so you know, we are full up on trolls already. It's not gonna be me." She followed the different paths, looking for the most recent swath of sparkling light. "A family of witches must have stopped here for a picnic a while ago." Their trails circled each other but the magic was fading.

Leira knelt down, running her fingers through a dark green trail that was all alone. "Bingo." She could feel the desperation in the fragments of magic left running along the ground, leaving an ache in her chest. "First time I think I've ever felt misery pass through me."

"That way." Yumfuck was standing up on Leira's shoulder, his arm outstretched. "He's that way." The troll trembled, his teeth clacking together. "He's losing his shit." Yumfuck grabbed onto Leira's collar as she took off at a run. "Turn by the big oak. Now!"

Leira followed the troll's directions, letting her own energy spread out in front of her as a backup. But it wasn't long before she heard the rooting and growling, and she slowed down. On the other side of a thick stand of trees the troll was banging against an old twisted tree. He was panting heavily and standing at his full eight foot height.

"He doesn't look good," said Leira. He was swinging his

head left and right, squinting up at the sun and bashing his arms against the trunk of the tree. "His sight is just about gone."

"Then we better find a magical host. He doesn't have long." The troll squeezed her collar harder, his teeth clenched."

"Find a magical host in the middle of nowhere who'd be willing to take on a half-crazed troll who's lost part of his essence. Fucktastic." Leira thought of one person, furrowing her brow. "Never thought I'd pull this one." She centered herself and sent out a stream of magic, searching for a connection. *I need your help. Come in person.*

The magic pulsed through her, rattling her bracelet. The injured troll slowed his beating on the tree and looked up, smelling the air. The leaves on the ground around them lifted into the air floating around their ankles.

Behind Leira a portal opened, and Jackson leaped through, an arrow already notched on his bow. "Where is it? Let me at them!"

"Dad, use your inside voice," whispered Leira, as the leaves settled back down to the ground. "And lower the fucking bow. It's not that kind of emergency. Geez, I've asked for your help when there's not an attack."

Jackson slowly lowered his bow and scratched his head. "No, no I don't think you have. You're usually just this side of splatter when you call me."

Leira rolled her eyes at him. "I don't think so. Fine. I'll do better and send out a magical hug once in a while." She took his hand and let her magic swirl around him. "Right now, I need your help with something."

"This can't be good. You're being very friendly. I missed the teenage years. I have no idea of your tricks."

"Not a trick. You remember Yumfuck. He's a great companion. Has saved my life so many times. Even saved *Mom's* life at least once. You remember Mom."

"You're laying this on pretty thick. You know you can't break your bond with the furry fella."

"Not trying to. He's invaluable to me."

The troll waved at Jackson, trying a big grin just as a growl went up from the brush.

"What was that?" Jackson lifted his bow again but Leira pushed his arm down.

"That's the big ask from your only child. Your long lost daughter that you love who worries about you living in the Dark Forest all alone."

"I have a dog."

"Yeah, and they're great but can they fight next to you in a battle? Maybe some, okay. But do they speak? Can they do intel?" Leira shook her head. "No, no they cannot."

"Fuck me. This has got to be bad. Did you hit something? Do I need to bring someone back from the near dead?"

Leira startled. "Wow, surprisingly close." Leira pulled her father by his hand closer toward the side of the clearing. "I need you to adopt a troll."

Jackson pulled back, his eyes widening at the sight of the tortured troll, stomping around on the ground, muttering to itself.

"What the fuck? That's still barely a troll! This isn't like you brought home a stray cat. That's an addle-brained troll on the verge of extinction. How about we put it out of its misery instead? That seems all around kinder."

Yumfuck hissed and growled at Jackson.

Leira tilted her head to one side. "This can be for all my birthdays up to now." She smiled, waiting for her father to answer. Hagan's rule.

"Wow, you do not play fair. You get that from my side. Fuck me," he said, shutting his eyes and muttering under his breath.

"What are you doing, Dad?"

He finally opened his eyes and looked into his daughter's eyes. "How can I tell you no? Fuck, when you call me Dad it sounds like music. A one syllable song that makes everything easier." He strapped the bow to his back and shook out his arms. "A fucking troll. You know it's for life."

"Yeah Dad, I know."

Yumfuck waved to him, rolling his eyes. "We all know."

"You'll barely know he's there."

"How do we do this?" asked Jackson.

"You don't know?"

Jackson's eyes grew wide again, and he started to sputter.

"Just kidding. Yumfuck knows. I'm trying to give you the whole teenage daughter experience, so you don't feel like you missed out." Leira patted her father on the back. "Heart speed up there?"

"Let's get a move on," said Yumfuck. "We're running out of time. Jackson has to be the one to calm him down and make contact with him. Physical contact. Then you let your energy flow through him till it takes. It's really kind of easy once you get past the contact part."

Jackson looked at the hulking beast running his claws through the bark and back at Yumfuck. The small troll shrugged and held out his paws. "Yeah, that part's hard but you're a Jasper Elf. You can do it."

"We'll help," said Leira. "We'll distract him. You can touch him from behind."

"Boy, that didn't sound right," said the troll.

Jackson shook his head. "Every birthday?"

"Yes, every single one of them. But I will expect a present next year, of course." She kissed Jackson on the cheek. "Love you, Dad."

Jackson had started to move but stopped and looked back at her, his eyes shining. "You've never said that before," he whispered.

"Yeah, well, I do. So, don't fuck this up. That would ruin a touching moment."

"I love you too, kid," he said and crept around to the left, behind the stomping troll. Leira and Yumfuck went to the right. They got to the edge of the clearing as Yumfuck scrambled to the ground, already growing to his full height.

The injured troll could see the shadows changing and roared, waving his large paws in the air. Yumfuck answered with a roar and a trill, beating his chest.

Leira stood by Yumfuck's side, the symbols along her arms rolling slowly over. She kept an eye on her father who was almost behind the troll as Yumfuck let out another roar followed by a trill.

The wounded troll answered by tilting back his head and letting out the same mournful howl Yumfuck had done when he saw the picture. He waved his arms in the air and bashed a fist into a tree.

"That's what a broken heart sounds like," said Yumfuck. He answered with a howl of his own.

Jackson reached out and grabbed the fur on the back of the troll, startling the tall beast. The troll spun around, shaking his large head, trying to swipe at his back but he couldn't reach. He swirled around and around, pulling Jackson off his feet and throwing him around behind him.

"This would be ridiculous if it wasn't so dangerous," yelled Leira. She sent out a ribbon of magic to her father with an intention. *Focus.*

Jackson grabbed on with his other hand and his eyes began to glow and the symbols along his arms lit up. His magic crept around the girth of the large troll, binding him slowly. Jackson's energy sought out all the broken ends of the troll's energy where he had been ripped away, weaving the two magicals together.

The pain became shared and Jackson gritted his teeth, but the joy Jackson felt also seeped over to the troll, calming him down.

"Wow," muttered Leira, at the circles of light that were spinning around the troll and her father. "They're bonding, it's working."

The light sped up, letting out a high pitched whine, ending in a *bang.* Jackson fell to his knees and finally let go of the troll, breathing hard from the exertion. The glow faded from his eyes as the troll turned around, shrinking down to just five inches tall. He crawled up on Jackson's knee and rested his head on Jackson's hand.

"Why do I feel like I gained a sibling?" Leira waited till Yumfuck shrunk down and scooped him up, putting him back on her shoulder. She came and crouched by her dad, looking more closely at the troll. "Purple hair. I can dig it. What are you gonna call him? What about Mick?"

"Or Joker!" chirped Yumfuck.

"Oh nice one," Leira laughed. "Wait, doesn't he already have a name?"

"That would have left too. Blank slate," said Yumfuck, shivering. "Everything is reset. Oooooh what about Norman."

"Norman? Why... never mind."

"He'll name himself in good time. Maybe we start with what happened to his first magical." Jackson picked up the troll and held him in his palm. He pushed himself off the ground and stood up, brushing off his knees. The small troll blinked hard a few times, clearing his eyes but some of the cloudiness remained.

"That's going to take a while," said Yumfuck. "But he should be able to see more already."

Jackson held him up where the troll could see him. "How'd you get separated from your last dance partner?"

The troll pressed his little paws to his face. "He was being taken away to someplace horrible. Someplace he didn't expect to survive." The troll pressed a paw against his belly, his eyes filling with tears. "Or maybe was hoping he didn't. He wanted to make sure I didn't go there too."

Leira rubbed the top of the troll's furry head. "What do you mean by horrible?"

The troll shook his head and clasped his paws to his chest. "Magicals have been disappearing. Some say they're doing experiments on them, like the old days." A shudder passed through the troll's tiny body. "But this is worse. A magical is taking them. One of our own would do something like that to us..." His voice trailed off.

Leira sat back on her heels, her heart pounding in her chest. "Do you know the name of the magical?"

"Wolfstan Humphrey," whispered the troll, scrambling up Jackson's arm and disappearing into a pocket. Jackson's shirt shook from the troll's trembling.

"That fucker is becoming a modern Rumpelstiltskin," said Leira, standing back up.

"We have to stop him," growled Yumfuck.

"We will," said Leira. "One way or another, we will." Leira hugged her father, startling him again. He smiled, wrapping his arms around her. "Wow, it only took bonding with a half-cocked troll, but I'll take it."

Leira opened a portal to her house and looked back at her father. "I promise I'll seek you out at least once a week just to hug you with a little magic."

"Best deal I've made this week," he said, as Leira stepped through and the portal gradually closed, leaving him alone with a troll, forever.

CHAPTER TWENTY-ONE

Correk stood in the kitchen in a Hot Tuna long-sleeved t-shirt and a new pair of jeans that Leira had picked out for him, munching from a bag of Doritos.

"Leira, we need to get going. Yumfuck is already there." There was no answer and he went down the hall, carrying the bag and leaned against the banister. "Are you listening? What are you doing up there?" Still no answer.

He left the bag on the top of the newel post and went up the stairs, taking them two at a time, his long braid swishing behind his back. "We're just going down the street," he said, as he started up the next flight and made his way down the hall to their bedroom door.

Leira stood in front of the mirror, pushing her bangs off her forehead. She was wearing a little black dress and sandals, turning to the right and the left.

"Are you wearing makeup? You were already beautiful."

"Good answer. I want to make a good impression. An entire building of older magicals. It's like an economy package of new friends."

Correk smiled and walked up behind her, wrapping his arms around her waist and resting his chin on her shoulder. A dangly gold earring swung against his cheek. "Jewelry even." He smiled at her in the mirror. "They're just neighbors. You were less nervous about meeting the Queen of the Light Elves."

"I always do better with hostile first impressions." Leira put her hands on her hips and turned her head to one side. "And I'm not living down the street from Queen Saria. I'm starting a new life in a new place."

"They will love you, just like Toni and the others do."

"It's not like I'm trying to replace them, but it is kind of funny."

"What is?"

"When I lived in Austin, it took ferocious battles for me to realize I had a family all along. It's like I have to start all over, and we both know I'm not the best at idle conversation."

"You always manage to get your point across."

Leira laughed. "I don't think swearing is going to earn their affection."

"Just be yourself. That's what you're best at."

"You realize we're going to a party based on an invite from our troll."

"Sounds about right. Now, come on... Grab the potato salad you bought and let's get over there. Yumfuck carried over fried chicken, and he's not going to save any for me. Hang on." Correk let go of her and stepped back. His phone buzzed as he slid it out of his back pocket. "It's my dad. It's Harkin."

Leira smiled. "I know who your dad is. Answer it."

"Still weird to get a call from him."

"Doesn't mean it's bad news."

"Hello?" Correk walked out into the hallway. "Harkin, everything okay? Yeah, we're fine. Leira's here, we're about to go have dinner at the neighbors. Yeah, normal life kind of stuff. What are you doing? Well, I've heard Rose is a pretty good cook. Don't let the Dryad feed you. Nuts and berries, all day long. How's that information working out? Did it help? Lily *is* really brave. She insisted on going back. No good, huh? Did it get you closer? Well, that's something. Let me know if you get the machine to work. Sure, Dad. I'll call you later."

Correk hung up and slid the phone back into his pocket as Leira came out into the hallway. "Lily's new research didn't quite work. I think Harkin got his hopes up, again. He sounds lonely."

Leira let out a sigh. "He got a taste of family and he liked it. That's a good thing. We should invite him over. I mean, now that his name's clear there's no reason not to."

Correk slowly nodded. "It never even occurred to me. Yeah, I guess you're right. We could have my dad over for dinner."

Leira rubbed his back. "We can take him to Soi 38 on L Street. Celeste has been raving about it."

"Celeste? You're making a lot of friends here. I knew you could do it."

"Mostly texting. They make it easy. I wish it was that easy to contact the Jersey Willen. You really think an ordinary rat could reach him?"

"Maybe. He's a smart Willen. He'll stay on the move."

"We can't let Wolfstan get that ring." She put her hands

on Correk's shoulders. "I'm letting that go long enough for a party. Time for you to let go of one thing. Text Harkin and invite him to dinner."

Correk pulled his phone back out. "First time I've felt like a normal son in... a hundred years. There, done. Now can we go? I'm starving. I'm out of snacks. Still haven't figured out how to keep Yumfuck out of my trove."

"Have you thought about buying Yumfuck his own stash?"

"He'd still want mine."

Leira smiled. "It's becoming a thing with the two of you." She turned and kissed Correk, lingering for a moment. "Start with buying extra. You spend less time worrying over a magical." She walked by him, heading for the stairs with Correk right behind her.

"Has Yumfuck let you in his room lately?"

"No, he keeps saying he needs his privacy." Correk glanced over at the troll's closed door as they took the second set of stairs down to the first floor. "I figured he didn't want me finding empty wrappers."

Leira looked back up the stairs. "Yeah..." *Or a permanent portal. No, trolls can't do that. Can they?* She shook off the notion and headed for the kitchen.

She pulled out the large plastic container from the refrigerator and scooped it into a yellow ceramic bowl, covering it with plastic wrap. Correk watched her with crossed arms. "Seems like a lot of trouble to make them think you cook."

Leira held up the bowl with a sheepish grin. "It's more I want them to think I'd bother for them. Frankly, for me this is really bothering. Okay, time to meet the neighbors. Put your game face on."

"This is the only face I have. It'll have to do."

"I love that face."

Leira grabbed her purse from the front hall and they went out the front door. They strolled down the street, Correk's arm around Leira's shoulder. The setting sun was casting a luminescent yellow glow over the brownstones along N Street and the sky had streaks of purple.

They got to the brownstone down the street and stopped in front of the building, looking up at the third floor. "We should go in," said Leira.

"Waiting on you. What would Estelle tell you right about now?"

"Get your ass in there." Leira squared her shoulders and started walking. Correk got ahead of her and held open the door. They took the two short curving flights and walked down the hall to apartment C. Music could be heard coming from the other side.

"Somebody knows their blues. That's Andrew Alli playing harmonica on *Hard Workin' Man*." Leira took a deep breath and knocked. "Here goes nothing."

"You're a Jasper Elf. If they try anything you can probably take them all."

"Very funny."

The door flew open, startling Leira and her face warmed as she tried to smile through it. Correk gave a squeeze to her shoulder.

"You must be Yumfuck's family. Come in, come in. I'm Marcy, that's my husband Emmett. Welcome to our home and to the neighborhood." She stepped back to let them in as Correk put out his hand. "Correk and this is..."

"Leira Berens!" Portia glided over, a drink in one hand, her other one waving, bracelets jangling on her wrist. "You are famous, young lady. Magicals know who you are, and you brought the Fixer! Now we can party, and the rescue is already here."

Leira gave a crooked smile as Marcy took the bowl from her and George appeared with two Port City Porters. "I'm George, married to Portia and the luckiest man around. Yumfuck said you like good beer. We already have that in common. This is a nice dark beer. A chocolate bomb. Stick with me. I'll make sure you try all the right beers before you die, or leave DC."

"I'm Elijah, the resident Wood Elf." He put out his hand to shake. "I'm the resident fix-it man if you ever need something."

"We need about a hundred things." Correk shook his hand, his mind wandering to Perrom and Ossonia. Leira put her hand on his back, her energy wrapping around him.

"How did you know about Andrew Alli? He's a great blues man," said Leira.

Emmett laughed as the others stepped out of the way. Behind them was the troll standing on a side table next to a record player. "That's Yumfuck's picks. He's playing deejay for us. Your troll has great taste."

A set of headphones were next to the troll and he was waving a paw over his head.

"He would be killer at weddings," said Leira.

"I said the same thing," said George. "Yumfuck said you were a detective in Austin?"

"Yeah, a homicide detective until I found out about my...heritage."

"No need to edit yourself. We're all magicals in this building. What are you doing in DC? I hear rumors that you're working for the Feds."

"George is retired from the Silver Griffins but he still likes to swap stories," said Portia. "Nudge him when you're tired of being questioned."

"I don't mind. I'm looking at my options." *The Silver Griffins know I met with the Senate panel. That's interesting.*

There was a "Whoop, whoop" from the far side of the room and

Stairway to Heaven started playing. Yumfuck was on his toes waving a lighter over his head.

Marcy came to the center of the room and waved a wand, the lights blinking. "All right, everyone, food is ready. Come and get it!"

Correk clapped his hands and strolled happily toward the kitchen. Yumfuck bounded off the side table and ran between feet, beating Correk to the food.

"What... hey!" Correk started to race the troll but Leira gave his arm a gentle tug and raised her eyebrows. "We can always get more," she whispered.

"I've been bested by five inches of fur."

"You can get there first with me, later," Leira whispered, giving a small bite to his ear lobe.

"Suddenly I'm the winner." Correk nodded to George and scooped a spoonful of the potato salad. "Oooh, pie."

Leira and Correk found two folding chairs near the door and balanced their plates on their laps, listening to George tell them stories from the Silver Griffins. The troll had pulled his overloaded plate over by the record player. He was happily sitting in the middle of his food, turning in a circle as he ate.

Leira took small bites, listening into different conversations and slowly feeling herself relax. *Roots really can be transplanted.*

It wasn't long before Correk and George wandered back for second helpings. Leira realized she wasn't watching the clock and she gave a crooked smile, laughing at one of Elijah's jokes.

Marcy stood and clapped her hands, getting everyone's attention. "Let's do some magical show-and-tell."

"Like the Jackalope," gasped Leira, wiping her hands on a napkin. Correk sat back down, three different slices of pie on his plate. He let out a contented sigh as Leira leaned her head on his shoulder.

"This is bliss," muttered Correk.

"I'm going to assume I figured into it."

"You're most of it."

"I'll take it."

"I'll go first." Marcy stood by the deejay booth, waving her wand in large figure eights. Monarch butterflies emerged one at a time, unfurling themselves from the tip of her wand. Wherever they landed, flowers appeared, blooming just as the butterflies took flight again.

"All right, my turn, and I promise no insects," said George.

George stood by the kitchen island, his chest out. He waved his wand in short jerky motions, throwing a cascade of sparkling blue light around the room. The light began to take shape, forming into a solar system that floated around each person.

"Star light, star bright..." cooed Yumfuck. He poked his furry finger into a twinkling star just above his head. Leira held out her hand, the light from Saturn bouncing off her skin. A comet swished by Correk leaving a sparkling trail.

George clapped his hands and the magical planetarium slowly faded, earning him a round of applause. "I've been working on that for a month," he said, beaming.

Portia got up next, giving George a high five as she walked to the center of the room. She swirled her wand over her head releasing a long trail of gray smoke.

Leira leaned forward excited, watching the smoke morph into a sinuous silver dragon. Ice crystals billowed out of its nose as it glided through the air, circling everyone, snowflakes dropping to the floor. Yumfuck stretched his arm up to run his finger across the scales and the dragon burped, frosting the tips of the troll's green fur.

Portia curtsied and went back to her seat next to George.

Everyone looked to Leira, but she was looking at Correk. He was suddenly distracted, his eyes moving back and forth. *I've seen that look before.* A magical was in trouble.

"We need to go, I'm sorry," said Leira, rising out of her chair. "Thank you for inviting us and being so kind to Yumfuck."

"Actually..." Correk stood, still distracted by the magical trails no one else could see. "I have a very big ask." He leaned closer to Leira. "It's Ossonia."

Leira put her hand on Correk, her eyes glowing. It was

faint, but it was there. Ossonia's energy was reaching out to them. "It worked," whispered Leira. "We made contact."

"We lost a friend to the world in between," said Correk, putting his plate down on the island. "There's not a lot of time to explain..."

"And it's okay to say no." Leira found her purse and slung the strap over her shoulder.

"We've gotten magicals out of that world before."

"My grandmother for one."

"But it takes a lot of magic to do it." Correk scooped up the troll, putting him in his pocket.

"A lot of magicals. There's a house not too far from here on New York Avenue that has a weak spot. A thin place between here and the world in between."

"I'll bet I know the house. Locals say it's haunted, but we always suspected a weak spot," said Emmett.

"If we can get enough energy pulsing toward the weak spot, we may be able to open a door while Ossonia is standing near it."

"She's there now? That's what you're sensing," said Marcy.

"It's her, I'm sure of it and the only way I'd be able to feel her energy in the mix of everyone else is if she's near a vulnerable spot."

"We may be able to grab Ossonia and finally pull her out." Leira's voice caught in her throat.

Correk squeezed her hand. "But it will take more than just the two of us." He bit his lip, waiting. Leira and Correk looked expectantly at the others. Yumfuck poked his head out of the pocket and reached out with his tiny arms.

"Of course we're in!" yelled George, punching the air. "A rescue from the world in between."

"I'll get my coat," said Marcy.

"Now that'll be a magic trick," said Portia.

"I don't think any of us will be able to top it." Elijah took one last bite of pie.

"Is there time to tell Perrom?" Leira was already marching out the door, not waiting for the answer.

"Meet me at the house." Correk was already opening a portal. "I can find him in time, but I can't guarantee he'll come back with me." The fronds of a large palm rustled in the breeze, poking into Marcy's home.

"The Dark Forest," sighed George, taking a deep breath of the sweet air. "It's been too long."

Correk stepped through and at the last moment, handed the troll back toward Marcy. "Protect Leira till I get back," he said to the troll. "Don't let her start without me."

CHAPTER TWENTY-TWO

Leira paced the room, the swells of energy coming from the shimmering air only making her heart race faster.

"He'll get here." Portia gently smiled as George walked around the shimmering air.

"Will you look at that? I've heard of the things but I've never seen one before."

"Don't touch it, George. We don't need to pull two magicals out of that goo." Emmett scowled standing toward the back.

"He's always been the most practical one of us," said Marcy. "It's probably saved our asses a few times."

"Each one of us helps the wheels go round on this group," said Elijah. "Marcy and me, we're most likely to run in first, read the directions later."

Leira managed a tight smile. "You're like me. Correk is the one who grounds me."

Sparks skittered across the floor and a portal opened. Leira leaned closer, holding her breath, her chest tight. The opening grew wider as Correk stepped through, a grim look on his face. Leira felt the heaviness of disappointment looking at the empty forest behind him.

But Correk looked back, yelling, "It won't stay open forever."

The Gardener of the Dark Forest came into view, the vines in his hair curling around his long locks. The tenants of the brownstone all stepped back, their mouths hanging open as the Gardener stepped through, holding out his hand for the Dryad. "Don't keep your mother waiting," boomed the Gardener.

At last, Perrom came and stood in the frame of the opening, his face hardened from grief. His body was slightly turned to the right, trying to hide the artificial arm attached at his left shoulder.

"If there's even a chance, Perrom," the Dryad said softly.

Perrom stepped through, ignoring Correk and making his way to one side of the room, further away from Leira.

Correk gave Leira a brief shake of his head and she felt the familiar ache that started in Paris settle into her chest again.

"The Gardener is real," muttered George, his eyes wide. He stood up straighter, watching the Wood Elf with fascination. "I mean I heard stories..."

"You know I can hear you," growled the Gardener.

"He forgets that sometimes," said Portia.

The Dryad smiled. "We are Perrom's parents and we loved... love Ossonia as one of our own."

"I'm Portia, a witch and this is my husband, George. We're all neighbors of Correk and Leira. I'm afraid we're at a disadvantage. We came barreling down the street with

Leira, but we don't know much about what we're doing here."

Leira started to speak but Perrom abruptly cut her off, pushing himself to the center of the room, staring at the shimmering air. "There was a great battle on the streets of Paris." He brought his fingers close to the shimmering air, creating sparks that hit the floor, leaving small burn marks. Perrom pulled his hand back, still watching the air. "There was chaos everywhere and people dying, magicals fighting. It went on for blocks. Shifters roamed the streets. Somehow in the middle of it all the world in between opened up, right there. The darkness in the place had come at last for Leira Berens but Ossonia pulled her back at the last moment and it took her instead."

Leira pressed her lips together, remembering every second of that night and Alan Cohen lying dead in her arms. *Another thing the Dark Families still have to answer for. Not today, but soon.* "There's so much of that night we can't fix. But this one thing, there is still a chance." She looked around at all the faces in the room. "I was in another room and not all that long ago. Room three-o-two of the Driskill Hotel. I was surrounded by magicals then too. They were willing to put themselves on the line to do something that had never been done before. To rescue my grandmother, a woman they had never met. Fuck, they barely knew me. Here we are again and Ossonia is like a sister. She was lost pulling me back." Leira's eyes were shining. "It was supposed to be me in there."

"Enough." Correk spit out the word. "No one should be in that hell." He moved swiftly surprising everyone, placing himself inches from his old friend, his face twisted in anger and pain. "You blame us for what happened. Arrogance," he growled. Perrom's cheek twitched in anger but he didn't move.

The troll jumped from Marcy's pocket and grew to his full height, a low, steady growl in the background.

"I will not let you keep saying that Leira's life matters less. Her life is everything to me." Correk's hands were clenched in fists at his side. The Dryad took a step, but the Gardener pulled her back. "Let him speak. No one else has been able to get through to Perrom."

"The darkness sought her out because she is made of light. That's not her doing." He pointed a finger at Perrom's face, the tight muscles in his arm flexing. "You know damn well that Leira would never *let* Ossonia trade places with her. It just happened. It's horrible. But if you can't let go of this self-righteous fury then you will be a part of the reason we never get her out."

Perrom's chest heaved up and down and he slowly shook his head. "Fools," he whispered. He shoved Correk aside and opened his hand, a ball of light already growing into a portal.

"Let him go." The Gardener's voice thundered in the bedroom, rattling the windows. "He's drowning in his own grief and until he wants help, there's nothing we can do for him. Ossonia is trying to find us. We can help her."

Perrom stepped through the portal, his head hanging down. He turned back as the portal closed, locking eyes with Correk. "It should have been Leira," he hissed, as the portal closed. Correk raced at him, tearing at the edges of the portal but it was already fading into nothing. Sparks danced around his feet.

Leira stepped in front of Correk, her eyes glowing and the energy pulsing through her. "Correk, it's just angry words. They can't harm me or you or anyone but Perrom. He's suffering in his own misery. The Gardener is right. We have to wait till he's ready." Leira took in a slow, even breath looking at the neighbors all standing together, holding on to each other. "Are you still in?"

"Honey, we are all the way in," said Portia. "We're just waiting for instructions."

"You know magicals," said Elijah. "We come together when the shit hits the fan. Well, most of us. No offense," he said, a nod to the Dryad.

"I haven't been on an adventure like this in about a hundred years," said George. "Phew!"

"Tell us what you need us to do, honey." Marcy stepped forward, her hands on her hips. "We're ready to go. We don't back down from fights. We never have and we're not starting now."

Leira squeezed Marcy's hand. "Yumfuck has always been a very good judge of character. Thank you. Well, if we're gonna do this, we need to join hands in one continuous line." Leira reached out for Correk's hand and went and stood in the middle, placing herself directly in front of the shimmering air. The others lined up with the Gardener and the Dryad next to Correk. At the end of the line was Yumfuck Tiberius Troll, anchoring all of them.

"Can you still sense her magic?" asked Leira, the symbols on her arm glowing brightly, flipping over again and again. The Gardener looked over at her arms, his brow furrowing. "You can tell the future," he gasped.

"You've managed to impress the Gardener," said the Dryad. "Already one miracle. Let's go for two."

Leira looked up and down the line. "No matter what happens, don't let go." She looked at Correk. "Tonight we fight with honor and to the end."

"If it's the last good thing we do." He leaned down and kissed her, mashing her nose. "Keep the bracelet on," he growled.

Leira didn't answer, pulling her head back.

"I know that determined look. Find another way," said Correk.

Leira took in a deep breath and let herself relax, the energy growing inside of her. *Find Ossonia, make a door.* The energy swirled around her feet, crawling up her spine and filling her chest. The scar on her belly burned from the flood of magic coursing through her. Her hands warmed as the magic began to spread down the line in both directions and her muscles grew tense.

The magic circulated through the room creating a vortex that ended in a spear of light jutting out from Leira.

Leira felt the energy reach out in front of her, probing at the shimmering air. She could hear Turner Underwood's advice. *Clear your mind. Let the magic do the work. Get out of the way.*

The energy made contact with the thin film between the two worlds, adding to the fuel that was already burning. Leira felt the light grow and a sense of peace come over her even as Correk squeezed her hand harder, doing his best to ground her.

BANG!

The shimmering air collapsed in on itself, imploding

into the world in between and with a bright flash blowing out toward the magicals in the bedroom. Marcy stumbled backward, loosening her grip but the magicals on either side of her held fast till she found her footing.

A loud renting tore through the opening creating a jagged edge. Grey, mottled hands appeared at once, reaching out into the room, grasping at the air. Portia gasped and took a step back, her eyes wide but she never let go.

Ossonia. Leira held the intention, trusting in the energy to do its work. A warmth surrounded her magic, adding to it and she realized the new Fixer was combining their power. Correk had grown stronger, wiser since that day in the Driskill Hotel. Leira could feel Ossonia's energy reaching out to them and she pushed harder as the tear grew.

Suddenly, a long slender hand appeared, a wide sleeve billowing down from the wrist as the body pushed through the others. Ossonia's face appeared, strained from the effort as she wrestled with the others to escape.

Leira lifted up onto her toes, her back arching as the light rushed through her, beaming out to Ossonia, encircling her. She heard Correk groan from the effort and felt a pain seeping into her joints. *Let there be enough magic. Please.*

Ossonia fought for her freedom, leaning out of the hole, her arms reaching for this world.

"Fuck me." Leira gritted her teeth at the sight of an old foe. Dark tendrils of heated mist were starting to curl around Ossonia's waist. The bedroom was filling with a rotten stank making Marcy wrinkle her nose. It pushed against the light as the arms of lost beings continued to fight, pulling at Ossonia.

Leira bore down even harder, the bracelet vibrating on her arm. *Pop!* An arm grasping at Ossonia exploded into ash, the remains dropping to the floor. *Pop! Pop!* Ossonia regained her position, freeing her chest.

But the dark mist grew, encircling her and more arms replaced those that were lost. Ossonia's mouth opened in surprise. She screamed out, "Perrom!" as hands clawed at her, pulling at her and in a flash she zipped backward, disappearing into the void.

Leira felt the remnants of Ossonia's trail leave Correk's magic so quickly it left an absence. Leira fell to her knees, her body shaking from the effort as the tear rapidly repaired itself and the shimmer disappeared. She let go and put her hands to her face, waiting for the pain to subside. "We've made it worse," she muttered.

Correk helped her stand and the others gathered around her, forming a tight circle, still holding hands. "We've made it worse," she said again.

"No, we only failed this time," said the Gardener. "We will learn from it and try again, as a team. That is the lesson I've failed to teach my son, but you know it, Leira Berens. Use it."

CHAPTER TWENTY-THREE

Turner Underwood stood undetected at the door of his movie room whispering an ancient spell that was directed at the contents of his favorite leather recliner. Leira stirred in the oversized chair, letting her aching body settle into the soft leather. Her mind was floating, soaring out of her body and out of Turner Underwood's large mansion. Everything was feeling peaceful, easier.

The old Elf stopped abruptly, turning his head. There was a soft click from the door that led to the hidden hallway. "Till we meet again," he whispered. Turner tapped his cane, disappearing in an instant.

Leira was just drifting off when Correk came back into the room. "Turner has an entire pantry just for movie snacks," he said, excited. Leira twitched, snapping back into her body, the soreness returning. She looked up at Correk, his arms loaded with Junior Mints, Sno Caps, and Reese's Cups. "What's happening?"

"I think I get the appeal to raiding someone else's stash." Correk sat down in the recliner next to Leira, candy sliding out of his arms. "Did you pick a movie? What about *Dirty Harry*? Yumfuck keeps quoting it."

"What the fuck? How are you this happy? You already ate a pile of that stuff." Leira sat up, looking Correk up and down. "All the signs of a sugar rush are there."

"It's nirvana."

"The same rules that apply to road trips apply to movies. You wait till the movie starts. That's a Nana rule."

"Here's a Correk rule. I eat it when I find it."

Leira laughed, wincing at the pain from the scar on her belly. "Oof. Do magicals need to go to the dentist? Come to think of it, I've never had a cavity."

Correk stopped opening the box of Junior Mints and took a better look at Leira. "Go back to sleep. I'll keep the sound down."

Leira settled back into the chair. "A compromise. Sounds good. After the movie you want to go to New York City from a hundred years ago? We could get some dinner. I love this house."

"Let's go back to Sea World."

Leira gave a crooked smile even as she started to drift off. Turner's spell was still lingering over her. "We keep getting naked under the sea and one of these days a mermaid is gonna catch us."

Correk leaned over and kissed Leira on the top of her head, sitting back in his chair. His eyes glowed for a moment and he opened his hand, sending a spiral of gold sparkles up in the air. "Play *Dirty Harry*." He reclined his chair, the candy shifting around him as the opening credits began to play on the ceiling. "I love this house too."

Lois made her way down the hallway of the Silver Griffins headquarters, the black patent leather purse dangling from her bent arm. "Ma'am? Ma'am!" Mabel Garner was hurriedly coming down the hall. Lois was lost in thought, ticking off her to-do list in her head. She tapped the side of her head and muttered, "That'd be a good one for Patsy. Oh, I'd better call Earl."

"Lois Filmore!" barked Mabel, her face warming. Lois stopped in her tracks, spinning around, the purse swishing back and forth. Mabel's gaze was entirely on the swinging gateway to the vault, even as she addressed Lois. "There's been an alert. A serious one."

Every stray thought left Lois' head. "Out with it." Her voice was firm and steady.

"Not here," said Mabel, looking around nervously.

Lois' forehead wrinkled and she tilted her head to one side, pulling the purse closer to her body. "Oh... I see." She pursed her lips and raised a finger, turning and walking away without another word. Mabel hurried to keep up with her and started to say something, but Lois glanced over her shoulder with a withering look.

"Right. Sure."

Lois looked back again, and Mabel put one hand over her mouth, picking up the pace. The head of the Silver Griffins stopped at a utility closet, opening the door. She stepped inside, not bothering with the light and headed straight for the loud furnace that took up most of the space. Lois took out her wand and tapped four screws in a pattern as a metal plate slid open and a beam of light poured out, surrounding the witch.

Mabel got to the door in time to see the light emerge and stood still, biting the inside of her cheek. Lois waited till the light dimmed and reached back, grabbing Mabel by the hand, pulling her into the fading circle.

Swoosh.

Mabel felt her stomach lurch as the pair were spun upside down and shrunk just before being sucked into the furnace. She watched the swirling colors, holding her breath, afraid and curious at the same time. They were promptly spit out the other side, right side up again.

Clink.

The metal plate on the furnace flipped back up again and the door to the closet swiftly closed, leaving no trace that anyone had ever been there.

The younger witch hiccupped repeatedly, her eyes wide, squeezing Lois' hands. "Oh my... what the... how did that..." She found herself standing in a glass cube floating in the same swirl of colors, not connected to anything.

"You can let go now. We're in a secure area. The most secure and can only be entered with me in tow. The Fixer set it up. We're not really anywhere, but we're here. What is the problem?" She smiled trying to encourage her new assistant.

Mabel patted her forehead, wiping off the sweat that was forming. "You shrunk a vault that was already inside a purse." Her head was spinning from the thought.

"It's the same theory, dear. Once you can do one, you can do an endless number. Focus on the task at hand."

Mabel stared back at Lois, blinking but not saying anything.

Lois snapped her fingers in front of Mabel's face, sending out sparks that caught Mabel's attention at last. "The message!" The words spilled out of the young witch. "Turner Underwood sent a message that he said I could give only to you in a secure area. He said you'd know what to do with it. *'The dots are connecting. Someone is hunting the lambs.'* That's all he said." Mabel shook her head and went back to biting the inside of her cheek.

Lois' smile froze. "Well, that is a pickle." Lois grasped her hands in front of her, the purse swaying. "What to do about a traitor?"

The color drained from Mabel's face and there was a ringing in her ears. "That's not possible. Is it?"

"My dear, you are a Silver Griffin standing in a floating cube on another plane in front of an old witch holding an entire vault up with just her arm." She raised her eyebrows. "Anything is possible." Lois' eyes moved back and forth as she thought out loud. "I suppose it was bound to happen again. There was that time back in the thirties when Rover Fleetwood was passing some of our secrets to the Nazis and was helping them march across Europe. Did you know it was the Dark Families that turned him in?" She wrinkled her chin. "No one liked the Nazis. Humorless butchers." Lois clapped her hands together. "Well, it's happening again. We will need to ferret out this turncoat. Mabel, tell no one. Never speak of this again anywhere. The walls can hear you in this place." She took a deep breath in and let it out slowly. "Patsy will be able to help us. She has a particular knack for smelling a bad seed. Until then, nothing else changes. Whoever it is can't know that we're on to them."

"What did Turner Underwood mean by someone is hunting the lambs?" Mabel shivered violently, her head shaking from the effort.

"The refugees from Oriceran. Someone has discovered the pipelines and is trying to kill them. Children, the elderly." Lois patted her hand. "Don't worry, dear. We'll find whoever it is and when we do, Trevilsom will be waiting for them. Come on, time to go back."

Mabel puffed out her cheeks, blowing out air. "Sure, I can doooooooo..."

The two witches were already spinning.

Clink.

The metal plate slid open, spilling them out and putting them back on their feet.

"I find it's best to go before you see the return visit coming," said Lois.

Mabel licked her dry lips, still swaying. "It feels like my brain was scrambled."

"Maybe a little."

"What?" Her mouth hung open.

"A little Silver Griffin humor, dear. You're fine. Go back to your post and get on with your day. Trust no one but me and make sure it's me before you do. If someone has figured out how to track the refugees, then we are dealing with a very clever renegade. It will take some doing to stop them before any real harm is done." Lois opened the door to the utility closet and left without another word and not looking back, the secret vault gently bouncing on her hip as she went back to walking down the hall.

CHAPTER TWENTY-FOUR

The Axiom offices were being kept to the same standard as if Charlie Monaghan were still showing up for work every day. Wolfstan Humphrey could appreciate that. He took a seat in the middle of the table content to at least look like a fellow among fellows. Pearson sat at the far corner watching Wolfstan with a half-bored expression, his fingers in the shape of a steeple pressing against his lips. It was only an act.

"Gentlemen and ladies, this shouldn't take long." The new CFO of the company, Jonathan Reardon, cleared his throat and pointed to the screen at the far end of the room. "Numbers for this quarter are very healthy, which frankly is a miracle after the debacle with Charlie Monaghan. The slight dip you see is from the payouts to the families of the men that were sent to Oriceran on an unfortunate artifact hunt. The good news is that we managed to get settlements with everyone, and nothing made the press."

"Who would have believed them if they did?" The

owner of a Swiss conglomerate sipped espresso from a delicate porcelain cup.

"No one in the public, everyone in the government," said Jonathan, "threatening many of our contracts with them." He glared at the Swiss owner taking a beat to make his point. "Then the sudden... retirement of Monaghan."

A murmur started in the room and people uncomfortably shifting in their chairs.

"You mean disappearance."

"I still say he's dead and buried under some new construction."

"Has anyone done an audit to make sure he wasn't doing some bologna slicing all these years?"

"He's got to be on some warm beach. Come on, it's Charlie Monaghan."

"What about that Langston fellow. Maybe he's seen him."

Pearson watched Wolfstan Humphrey and saw the edges of his mouth curl into a slight smile. *I'm watching a snake swallow a bunch of unsuspecting rats.*

"Everyone done with their speculating?" Jonathan had a sour look on his face. "Every major conglomerate in the world is represented at this table." He nodded in Wolfstan's direction. "Fleeker is our newest member. Keep your attention on what matters. The bottom line. The rest is a distraction and trouble. We've had enough of both to last for a while. The various governments are going to work with us as long as it's in their best interests. That stops the moment our connections to Oriceran are exposed to the public." He pressed his hands to his chest. "We know that what we're doing is for the general good in the long term. But it'll take years for the man on the street to catch up with that thought."

Wolfstan raised a hand, the large gold ring on his finger catching the light. He waited patiently till Jonathan called on him and then slowly stood, nodding to various board members. He came to Pearson and lingered a moment, one side of his mouth curling.

Pearson stared back at him, giving away nothing. A tendril of magic crept across the table unseen by everyone else, testing Pearson. He flipped his hand under the table, twisting the magic, yanking on it. The equivalent of a magical wedgie. Wolfstan's body jerked ever so slightly and Pearson saw the flash of rage light up his eyes before Wolfstan could gloss over it.

He had poked the monster.

Good. It may be the only way to throw him off. Pearson ignored the delight that had risen in his throat.

"I have a thought." Wolfstan was trying to sound congenial but there was an icy edge to his voice. He glanced back quickly at Pearson.

Thin skin, large ego. He is thrown off. This should be interesting. Pearson kept the same disinterested look.

Wolfstan opened his hand, allowing his eyes to glow and a flame to dance in his palm. "Someone who really understands magic..."

Several of the attendees moved away from him reflexively with worried expressions.

"And understands how to run a large, successful multinational business..." Wolfstan blew gently into his hand, the blue flame spreading out over the table, gliding across papers without burning them. People pushed away aghast, some standing nervously. Pearson moved back a few inches even though he knew the flame was harmless. A child's magic trick.

"Can negotiate the best deal with all sides. There is no true leader anymore. Not since Charlie Monaghan left and there are other alliances that are trying to make the same deals we are." Wolfstan took in a slow, steady breath as the blue flame pulled back, entering his mouth and lighting up his eyes with a blue glow for a moment. "Jonathan has the right idea, after all. Focus on the bottom line. Use every advantage at our disposal. Lack of information in a business deal can be deadly." He spit into his hand and threw his hand up, the same blue flame now broken into bits, reappearing as twinkling stars across the ceiling.

Suddenly I'm at a fucking kid's party and Wolfstan is the magician. "What do you get out of the deal?" Pearson said the words slowly, ignoring the constellation above his head. "I mean, for all your extra effort I assume you'll want something."

"Only what Charlie Monaghan received. The opportunity to direct which deals, but unlike Charlie I understand Oriceran and the risks, as well as how to do business here, on this planet. I can guarantee you'll all still go home at night." Wolfstan shrugged. "Think of me as your secret weapon and a warrior of sorts, protecting all of you as well as the business interests."

The German leader, dazzled by the light show, was about to start a motion when Pearson cut him off. "Bring us a proposal of your ideas. Let us look them over and then we'll vote."

It was Wolfstan's turn to quietly glare at Pearson, sucking in his cheeks. "Of course, a wise decision and a simple one. I can have it ready for you in a week."

"Perfect. Then we're done for the day." Pearson got up, gathering his things. "I may have time for a little lunch before my next appointment." He left without looking back and kept going till he was safely inside the back seat of his black Lincoln Continental.

"How did the meeting go?" asked the young wizard assigned to him as his driver for the day.

"Mixed reviews." Pearson got out his phone and typed in the secure number for Lois Filmore. "Hello, you were right. He made a play to take over the business dealings. It may still work."

"He was defeated in Oriceran. We can do the same," said Lois. "Just take it Patsy. We can get more. Sorry, you were saying…"

"I hope you're right but I'm not willing to say that yet. Have you seen the beast up close and personal?" The car turned near the Capital, the familiar dome coming into view.

"I haven't had the pleasure."

"I think he knows who I am. It's getting more dangerous. You'd better have my replacement ready just in case something happens to me. Either way, stop Wolfstan Humphrey from getting control because God help us all if he does."

Lois hung up the phone and pushed her glasses back up her nose. A dull headache was settling into her head.

"Maybe... No..." Patsy was hovering near the plastic bins of candy fretting over what to try. Lois rolled her eyes and picked up her wand, flicking it in a small arch, zapping Patsy with a pea-sized fireball.

"For the love of..." Patsy whipped around and turned an M&M into a projectile, catching Lois on the side of her head.

Lois screwed up her face and circled her wand, lifting a pile of Starburst into the air to rain down on Patsy's head.

"Candy should never be weaponized!" Patsy gasped and started laughing. "If your underlings could see you right now, they'd worry about the whole organization."

Lois let out a guffaw. "They could all use a little more fooling around. Magicals walk around here with a scowl like it's some kind of uniform." She shook her head, her bouffant staying perfectly in place. "I suppose it's too soon. We'll have to ease them into our style."

Patsy looked around at the floor. "Thanks for not sacrificing the peanut M&Ms."

"I know where the line is. Thanks for helping me relax even if it was only for a minute."

Patsy pushed three M&Ms into her mouth, chomping down on them. "Hmph, tough times ahead."

"A traitor, a killer and a madman. And I have to worry about my niece. It's a lot."

"Not our first dance, though. We'll give them all what for, and when we're done Sirius and Wolfstan Humphrey will pay for all they've done." Patsy circled her wand near the floor, gathering the Starburst into a slowly rotating cyclone. She flicked her wand to the right, sending a strawberry toward Lois. "Chew on that and we'll devise a plan."

Lois unwrapped the pink candy. "First," she said, "we find a rat."

CHAPTER TWENTY-FIVE

Lily Sharpton sat on the shuttle winding its way into the tall gates of Fleeker and down the main drive. She kept herself buried in her book, *The Adventures of Maggie Parker*, and for good measure wore headphones playing scores by John Williams. The Star Wars theme song was blaring in her ears, helping to boost her courage. The two male engineers on the seats next to her were laughing and retelling their exploits from the night before, occasionally jostling Lily. *It was my choice to come back*, she reminded herself. *The job wasn't done.*

She looked up as an elbow caught her in the side and the offender said, "Sorry," immediately going back to outlining how he won at darts, talking with his hands. Lily glanced out the window at the elaborate flower beds in the circle as they neared the front entrance. *I loved this place.* She let out a sigh, her hands still grasping the book. The music changed to the low notes from Jaws, slow at first but rapidly sounding out faster and faster. They matched Lily's heartbeat as she stepped off the short bus.

Lily followed the others in, holding out her arm for the green light to read the chip. She walked to the elevators, the music getting faster, clutching the book to her chest.

Claire came bounding over, a bright pink headband with pearls along the top holding back her wild brown curls. "Hey, want to stop for coffee before we head up?"

"What?" Lily took off the headphones, pushing on the side to pause the music. She forced herself to smile and take long, slow breaths just like Leira had shown her. Keep the breathing steady and even. *It'll help trick the body into thinking everything is okay. Keep me hidden.* "Sure, I could use another hit of caffeine."

Claire bounced alongside her as Claire waved to the others in the open elevator. "I'll catch another one." The young man holding the door let go and went back to nudging his friend.

The two bioengineers walked toward the Starbucks tucked in a room behind the elevators. "Did you get the memo?" asked Claire. "We already have so many layers of security. Come on, at some point it's gotta be enough. I mean, I know we're working on cutting-edge stuff but…"

Lily squeezed Claire's arm to stop the stream of words. "What memo?"

Claire smiled and rolled her eyes. "You need to check your email more often." Claire scrolled through her phone and held up the email. "They've hired extra guards to walk around on the different floors now. They're supposed to blend in and not disturb anyone. Do you think that's to make us relax and do our work, or relax and do something dumb? I mean, before you know it, they'll be in the bathrooms with us."

Lily felt a cold sweat on the back of her neck. She sucked in air between her teeth and held her breath for a moment before slowly blowing it back out again. *Breathe.* Her mind was racing, trying to think of what to say next. "I wonder if someone's discovered something big. You know, like this is good news."

"Ooooh, I hadn't thought of that." Claire stepped up to the counter. "A grande oatmeal honey latte blonde espresso with one shot of caramel. Lily what do you want? I'll get it."

Lily was doing her best not to look around the room for extra guards. "Uh, a tall Americano." *That guy is new. He looks like he could be a guard. Is he a magical?* She was dying to send out just a little magic to check. But if anyone in the room was a magical, they would know she did it.

"That's it? That's almost like getting black coffee." Claire set a large oatmeal raisin cookie on the counter. "This too," she said, waving her wrist in front of the reader. The chip connected with the register that let out a sharp, metallic *ping*. "Here." Claire handed Lily her Americano, slipping her cookie into her pocket. "Hey, I'll bet we can guess who's a guard." Claire grabbed a straw to put in her coffee, sucking on the end.

Lily blanched, trying to recover and lifted her eyes even if her chin was still tucked. "What about that guy," she said, pointing to a man in a tight polo shirt.

"Him? That guy's in accounting. I know, doesn't fit the stereotype. Who ever heard of an accountant that likes to work out that much? I think his name is Stan or maybe it was Dan."

They headed out the doors and toward the elevators. Claire was biting her lower lip, studying a young man in a neat suit, waiting patiently by a different bank of doors. "Now that could be one of them. I haven't seen him before, and he looks like he's trying to fit in something fierce. Either that or he's here for an interview." The elevator doors opened, and a woman emerged, smiling brightly at the young man, holding out her hand and pulling him into the elevator with her. "Ah, interview." Claire shrugged, not noticing Lily wasn't saying a word.

"This could be fun," said Claire, slurping up more coffee.

Their elevators doors finally opened, and the pair stepped on, moving to the back as others crowded in front of them. Claire giggled and smiled at Lily who smiled back, quietly sipping her coffee. Lily waited till Claire looked away to release just a little magic to wind around the other six people. Only one was magical and no trace of darkness. The Light Elf looked up from his phone, confused and glanced around trying to see who was practicing magic inside the building. Lily turned to whisper to Claire, holding up her coffee cup. "What about him?"

Claire looked at the man, who scowled at her, pressing his lips together. "That's a lawyer from the ninth floor. Strange fellow. He always hurries through the cafeteria line and then takes his tray upstairs. His admin returns it for him."

"Getting off," said Lily in a loud, firm voice. The doors opened on their floor and the two girls pushed their way through the throng, doing their best not to slosh coffee. They hurried toward the double doors, drinking down the rest of the coffee. No drinks would be allowed past the first set of doors.

"Nobody out here," said Claire. "I guess they still trust us."

"Probably would be hard to hide someone on these floors. I mean, you can't accidentally wander into our section. A lot of floors are like that."

The doors opened with a soft whoosh and Lily found her locker putting away her purse and tossing the coffee cup. She put on the booties and gown, slipping a paper hood over her hair. Claire was still talking as they went through the second set of doors, making their way to their stations.

"There you are!"

Lily turned at the sound of her manager's voice, surprised to see her in their lab with a young woman next to her. Normal procedure was to call them to her office where no one had to wear a plastic face shield or goggles.

"We have someone new joining us today." The manager pointed a gloved hand. "This is Isabel. She's a new bio engineer and will be floating around for the first few weeks getting to know our procedures. This week she'll be in our department. Please be accommodating when you can."

"Finally, another female," whispered Claire. "Science nerdettes rock."

"Yeah…" muttered Lily, smiling. *Is this a guard? Would Wolfstan go to that much trouble? Maybe I'm overthinking it.*

"Isabel, your seat will be next to Billy, across from Lily. There's an iPad at your station that is checked out to you already. Wave your chip over it and that will unlock it. Instructions will appear to walk you through everything else. Lily?" The manager waved a blue gloved hand at her. "Can I speak to you for a moment?"

"Sure," nodded Lily, slipping by Isabel. She felt a sharp twitch of energy as she brushed past the new employee. Too short to be sure what it was, but it was there. Lily didn't dare look back in case it was a test. She got to her manager, keeping her back to everyone else. *Let it unfold. Breathe.*

"Your experiment looked so promising. I understand it's hit a roadblock. It's like you got to that very last inch and something happened."

"I'd like to continue testing, if that's amenable. There are a few more avenues to pursue."

The manager pursed her lips. "You're one of our best and brightest, Lily Sharpton. I'll give you just a few more days, but our budget can only take so much. If it's a failure we have to be willing to admit defeat and move on."

Lily nodded quietly and went to her chair, sliding behind her tray of slides.

"Rough week so far?" Isabel smiled behind the mask, tucking a blonde curl back under the paper hood.

"It's part of the job description. You have to fail a thousand times before you succeed. You must know that by now if you got a job here." She held Isabel's gaze, determined to look brave even if she didn't feel that way. "What do they have you working on?"

"Learning the ropes so far. Kind of boring. Maybe we can grab lunch together later?" Isabel sighed, fogging up her face shield. Her face reddened and she blinked a few times, uselessly waving a hand in front of her face.

Newbie mistake. She didn't spray her mask. Who are you? Lily typed a note to herself on her iPad, doing her best to ignore Isabel.

"Oh, I'd love to," chirped Claire from her station. "You'll want to avoid the salad bar. Ronald on the third floor uses his hand sometimes. The hot bar is okay but you're better off ordering something."

Lily smiled, ducking her chin and pulling out a slide. Sometimes Claire's effervescence came in handy.

Claire easily carried the conversation as Lily got to work, finally relaxing into her day and forgetting everything else for a while.

Hours passed and as people came and went, Isabel was watching everyone's movements.

Friend or foe, thought Lily. *Are you watching because you're new or something else entirely?* She lost herself in her experiments again, making notes and trying different things. She knew none of it would work, but it was necessary to look thorough. All along, in the back of her mind a thought was growing. *Keep Isabel close and find out more.* She purposely went down a rabbit hole, trying a different formula as she looked through her microscope at the results. The hair on the back of her neck stirred as she stared at the results. *How is that possible?*

"Time for lunch," declared Claire, standing up and stretching her back.

Lily looked up and checked the time on her iWatch as her stomach growled. "I could eat." She did her best to look calm, typing in the notes of what she had done before she could forget it. She licked her dry lips, checking her work and sat back.

"Come on, there's tacos today. I don't want to be late," said Claire, standing near the doors.

Lily waved her chip over the iPad and locked it. *It can*

wait till we get back. She got up to leave and went and stood by Claire.

Isabel got up from her station, carrying her iPad and made her way over to the two women.

"You'll need to leave that here," said Claire. "We can't take them in the cafeteria. These iPads have very sensitive info on them. That's why they all have an air gap. No internet. No way to send or receive. They told you that, right?" Claire's forehead wrinkled.

"Oh, yeah, of course they did. First day jitters, thanks," said Isabel laying it down next to Lily's iPad.

Claire seemed to let it go, already talking about the day's specials, but Lily wasn't going to be so easy. Something was off.

Lily followed them out stopping by the doors. "I have to make one more note before I forget. I'll catch up."

"Okay," nodded Claire, sitting down on one of the benches. Isabel was already taking off her protective gear and smiled at Claire.

Lily went back to her station, sliding Isabel's iPad away from her own. She waved her chip over her screen, unlocking it and went to the control panel looking for any recent additions. *Nothing.* She scrolled down further and was about to put the iPad down when she noticed an extension on a harmless search engine. *Wait a minute.*

She tried to delete it but was denied. The young witch tapped a finger on the screen, frustrated. She typed in a short string of code and gasped when she realized the new program was recording every keystroke she made and has sent half to another location before it was abruptly cut off.

Lily looked up at the iPad she had pushed away. Her

thoughts were spinning as she quickly checked the date on the added program. Yesterday. Isabel wasn't installing software. She was pulling data. Someone else had already come in and set Lily up to be caught.

"I knew it was you."

Lily looked up, her eyes wide. Isabel was standing at the end of the stations dressed in street clothes.

"You can't be in here like that. You're risking millions of dollars in research and thousands of hours of time." Lily did her best to sound angry and not scared.

Isabel slid out a wand. "You're a witch, right? I felt it when I brushed past you. You know how they caught you? Tiny little gaps in your chip's timecard. You were one place and then there would be a few seconds missing, maybe not even that long, and you were somewhere else."

"Witch? Is that some new millennial way of calling me a bitch? Not a great first impression." Lily felt inside her pocket for the blue marble Correk had given her. Maybe it could work again.

"Really? We have to play games? Alright," shrugged Isabel. "Have it your way. I'll bet when they analyze all those keystrokes, they'll find something strange." Isabel shook her head, walking closer, waving her wand in a figure eight. "Like you did find something?"

"Star light, star bright," whispered Lily, her hand grasping the blue marble in her pocket.

"A children's nursery rhyme? Surely you can do better than that." Isabel pointed her wand, opening her mouth to start a spell.

"First a star, and then make it night." Lily covered her face with her arm as a bright, pulsing light shot through the lab, blinding Isabel. It pulled back just as quickly sucking all light with it, leaving them in complete darkness. Lily kept her hand around the marble, still able to see in the dark as she moved to the other side of the table.

"You fucking bitch!" Isabel angrily waved her wand around, not sure where to point it. Sparks flew out the end taking out microscopes and glass jars, pouring different chemicals onto the floor and mixing them. Lily ducked under the spray of hot sparks, holding her breath as Isabel began to cough, holding her throat.

Alarms went off in the building as Lily raced toward the doors before it was too late.

Click!

The doors automatically locked down, trapping Lily in the lab without any way out. She squeezed her eyes shut, trying to think of another way out when two strong hands grabbed her by the arms. She opened her eyes in a panic, ready to fight when she saw Correk's face close to hers. "Time to go," he whispered.

Lily shook her head hard, pulling away. Correk held onto her but she pointed at the iPads, shaking her finger at them, still holding her breath. He let go and she scooped up both iPads as he opened a portal.

They stepped through as the doors opened and Wolfstan Humphrey stood on the threshold, his face twisted in anger in the returning light. Correk locked eyes with him as he quickly closed the opening, sparks dancing around his feet and the smell of chemicals lingering in the air. They were safe in his kitchen.

Lily ripped her mask off, gulping in air, clutching the

iPads to her chest. "How did you know?" she gasped, sweat covering her face.

"The blue stone. It sends me a signal whenever it's in use. I knew you had to be in trouble."

"I think I'm fired. Here, give these to Harkin. They should help him get the rest of the way. It corrects his formula and should make his machine work at last. I found it by accident. I wasn't even looking…"

Correk cut her off, wrapping his arms around her and lifting her off her feet in a bear hug.

"What are we celebrating?" Leira came into the kitchen wearing a dress and holding a bouquet of flowers.

"A miracle," shouted Correk, putting Lily back down. "An unexpected miracle."

Leira gave a crooked smile. "The best kind. Tell me more."

CHAPTER TWENTY-SIX

Correk stood at the open door watching his father tinker with a small engine, swearing under his breath. "Of all the insufferable, inanimate… Two moons!" Harkin grunted, trying to use a wrench to get off a stubborn piece, giving up and letting out an exasperated grumble. Correk smiled, his heart beating fast, reliving all the years he thought the man was dead.

"Dad."

Harkin tried the wrench again, straining from the effort, his eyes glowing as he tried to add in magic. "How is that even possible? Is there such a thing as magical super glue?"

"Dad." Correk said it a little louder, smiling. He watched Harkin take in a deep breath and flex his hands, working his fingers. The tips of each finger giving off a purple glow. "Come on Bessie, I know you can do it."

Correk swallowed hard, watching his father. He was feeling the loss of all the years. Mixed with it was gratitude for what was reclaimed. *What will this new information mean to all of us? One way to find out.*

"Dad," he shouted, startling Harkin who dropped the engine, the gear falling off when it hit the floor and rolling under the bench. Harkin blinked a few times looking at the engine and the gear. He looked at Correk, a surprised look on his face. Suddenly he tilted his head back and let out a roar of laughter, his entire body shaking.

A memory came back to Correk that he hadn't thought about in years. It was practically forgotten and in bits and pieces. But all at once there it was in a complete form. Correk was a young Light Elf watching his parents in their kitchen. His mother was hovering over Harkin, giving him directions to help fix a leak. It wasn't going well and Correk had watched, tense, waiting for his father to finally snap at his mother.

Instead, he had let out the same deep breath, going at it one more time. But the hole had only gotten bigger, shooting water straight into Harkin's face. His mother had clamped her hands over her mouth as Harkin wiped his face off with his shirt. He had looked at the shooting water and at his wet shirt and tilted his head back, letting out a roar of laughter. Correk's eyes shined as he blinked a few times, wiping his face on his sleeve.

"Dad, I have something for you."

"Is it food? I'm hungry for a good burger. Felix introduced me to them. They're amazing! Rose doesn't think either one of us should be eating them but..."

Correk went and wrapped his arms around his father, holding him tight, the words caught in his throat.

"What's this? Correk are you okay?" Harkin put his

arms around his son, patting him hard on the back. "Whatever it is, we can face it together. With honor and to the end."

Those words.

He had forgotten what it was like to be in his father's arms. Correk swallowed again and let go, stepping back. "Dad, I've brought you something." He took the iPad out of his satchel and handed it over. "Do you know how to use one of these?"

Harkin took the iPad and turned it over in his hands then smiled slyly at his son. "I made a machine that can alter DNA. I think I can figure out a bougie computer."

Correk took a piece of cloth out of his pocket and unfolded it, revealing a small chip. "You'll need this. I cut it out of a very brave young witch. You'll need it to unlock the computer. Once you have what's on there, destroy the chip. It was made by Wolfstan Humphrey. There's no telling what it can do."

Harkin held up the chip, turning it over. "At the least it's a sophisticated tracker. What's on the iPad."

"The thing you want most in this world."

Harkin's brow furrowed. He passed the chip over the iPad and went to the home screen. Correk leaned over him and touched the folder marked, *For Harkin*, opening it. Harkin's eyes scanned the material, his eyes growing wider with every line and his cheeks becoming flushed.

"Lily Sharpton swears this time it will work." His father grimaced but kept reading.

"Maybe, uh huh. Maybe." Harkin wandered off with the iPad, no longer paying attention to his son. Correk smiled, remembering that about his father too. "I'll be back to check on you, Dad. I have to get to the neighbors with Leira. Dad?"

Harkin was muttering to himself, pacing back and forth.

"Dad," barked Correk, startling Harkin again, but this time he held onto the iPad.

Correk laughed, rubbing his palms together. "I have to go. Leira is waiting for me, but I'll be back soon to see how it went. I'll come in person."

"Love you, son," said Harkin, smiling, his attention drifting back to the screen in his hands.

Correk smiled as he opened a portal. "Love you too, Dad," he said softly, before stepping back into the hallway of his house.

Leira was waiting, a ribbon now tied around the flowers. "How did it go? Was he excited?"

"You look beautiful," said Correk, taking her by the hand and twirling her around the kitchen.

"Thank you, you've said that already today. Did the information work?" Leira stopped spinning, leaning into Correk and kissing him, her tongue sliding between his teeth. He cupped the back of her head, closing his eyes, relishing the moment.

"If it was bad news, you're taking it really well," said Leira.

"It's too early to tell, but it looks hopeful. Very hopeful."

"Wow, I can't wait to see what you're like when it does work."

Correk laughed, kissing her again, running his hand down her back. "It's not that. I stood there watching Harkin and realized I missed him. It was painful and yet, some missing piece of me fell into place again." He kissed her again.

"Maybe we don't have to be the first ones to get to the Moss' party." Leira put the flowers down on the counter, taking Correk by the hand and leading him toward the stairs.

"I've always liked a good entrance," he said, following her up the stairs.

They passed Yumfuck's room just as something heavy hit the floor in his room. Correk stopped, staring at the door.

Leira looked back and yelled, "You're not tearing holes in the walls, are you?"

"No," came the muffled chirp from the troll.

"Let it go," said Leira with a shrug. "Whatever it is he's conjuring, it can wait. We have better things to do."

CHAPTER TWENTY-SEVEN

Correk and Leira stood at the front door of the Moss house, flowers in hand. Correk leaned over and brushed down the back of Leira's dress as she knocked. "Your dress was stuck in your underwear."

Leira's eyebrows went up. "That would have been a conversation starter. Totally worth it of course."

The door opened with Angel in mid-sentence, her arm wrapped around Nicole. "I would love to do an Undercover Wear party. We can have it here. Leira! You made it and you brought this big man with you. Are these for me? Love them, I'll put them in water."

Leira smiled at the wave of words washing over her. Nicole leaned in and gave Leira a hug. "Hey girl, come on in. Wine is cold and the gossip is getting hot."

Correk arched a brow, smiling at Leira. "You have come a long way," he whispered. "You're one of the girls."

"How do you even know that phrase?"

"Real Housewives."

Leira's eyes widened as Nicole led her away to the kitchen with Angel trailing them.

Matt came up to Correk with a tumbler of whiskey. "I hear you like a good bourbon." He raised his glass. "Here's to good neighbors." Correk raised his glass and took a sip, letting the warm liquid roll down his throat.

"I'm not sure I ever said thank you," said Matt. "I wouldn't have been able to help Ethan."

Correk shook his head. "Just doing my job. That was a temporary fix. We still need to figure out how he was poisoned."

Matt raised his glass to take a sip and Correk noticed the grey streak on the elbow of his jacket, a slight tear in the fabric. "Rough day at work?"

"What?" Matt rolled his arm, looking at the elbow. "Damn, I thought I got away clean. I went to take out the trash and some jerk on a motorcycle came peeling down the alley. Almost took me out. Don't tell Angel. That kind of thing really gets her going and she's already having nightmares from when I was attacked."

Correk looked over at the cluster of women, the dimples in his cheeks deepening at the sight of Leira talking, her hands moving through the air. *If Estelle could see you now. Or Hagan. Or anyone.*

Matt put down his arm, but when he did the light bounced off something shiny clinging to the back of his hand. Correk's smile faded and he grabbed Matt's arm, raising it to get a better look. "What's that.?"

"I don't know. I can't get it off. I've washed my hands a few times, but it won't come off. Angel thinks it's some kind of industrial glue."

"How about we go stand on your back porch for a minute?"

Matt stopped mid-sip, his glass still in the air. He lowered it slowly and looked down at the shiny patch on his skin. "Okay. If you think it's necessary. I can tell Angel I'm checking the keg."

"Just to be cautious."

Matt's jaw worked left and right as he gripped his glass. He jerked his head to the right and went past Angel kissing her on the top of her head. "I'm gonna introduce Correk to a boilermaker," he said, not stopping.

"Now it's a party!" whooped Celeste, holding her beer in the air.

Leira watched them go, making eye contact with Correk. She kept the smile on her face but quickly finished her beer. "I'll be right back. I want to know more about the thrupple down the street."

"I can barely handle one man," said Norah. "Why would anyone want two at the same time?"

Leira made her way outside, making sure to pour a beer in case anyone was watching. "Everything okay?"

"I think I know how the shifter was poisoned. Show Leira your hand, Matt."

The color drained from Matt's face. "You think this is the same shit that got Ethan? That means I could shift at any moment."

"How long ago did that biker try to mow you down?"

"I don't know, about an hour. Maybe?"

Correk tucked his hair behind his ears. "Ethan thought it was about that long when he started to shift. We need to get you out of here."

"Maybe not. I was talking to Turner," said Leira, "and I have a theory. But to test it, we'll need to go over to our house where there aren't any prying eyes."

"Let's just do it." Sweat was forming on Matt's forehead. "I can more easily come up with an excuse for that, than why there's a large wolf running through the house."

"Then you'll need to take my hand when we get closer. It's the only way you'll get through our wards." Leira stepped off the porch into the alley as the others followed her. "It's me or Correk. I'm okay with either one." She held out her hand as Matt took it and they passed through the magic fields to her back steps with Correk behind them.

Leira went into the kitchen just as the troll jumped off the counter, his arms full of Cheetos bags. Correk came in the door just in time to see Yumfuck running down the hall, headed for the stairs.

"You have a troll! That's the little kid we heard," said Matt.

"I knew it!" Correk barreled down the hall, giving chase but the troll was already at the next floor, turning the corner for his room.

"Are they bonded?" asked Matt.

"No, they both belong to me. Hello, their names are Correk and Yumfuck and they have a junk food problem. Or a sharing problem. I'm not sure at this point." Leira went to the banister and looked up at Correk. "Now how dumb do you feel? You just chased a five inch fur ball up the stairs to get back orange crunchy dust."

Correk reluctantly came back down the stairs. "It's the principle of the thing."

"What principle. You're the Fixer, you know, and we

have an oblempray in the itchenkay. Maybe we do that first."

"I'm circling back to this."

"I'm sure you are."

They came back in the kitchen to find Matt frantically trying to scrub off the goo at the kitchen sink. "It's not working."

"It's not going to," said Leira. "I think Wolfstan has figured out how to create a different plane of existence on a very small scale. Like a patch of skin or more accurately, a transferable sticky gel. That poison is here, but it's not here. I know, it's freaky. It's crossing over two planes of existence acting as a poison and altering shifter DNA. Normally, it would also be just about impossible to stop until it actually transferred."

"And then my spell could help shift him back," said Correk.

"Exactly but not before maybe a little mayhem and some exposure. I don't know, Wolfstan may be up to some bigger plan as well. It's hard to say yet. But there's something he forgot or maybe doesn't even know. I'm a Jasper Elf with a spark of humanity and my magic can cross planes." Leira gave a crooked smile.

Matt's mouth fell open as he stared at Leira.

"Dude, that's my girlfriend."

Leira shot Correk an amused look, pulling Matt into the hallway away from any windows. "You ready?"

Matt looked down at his arm and saw wiry brown hair sprouting. "Hurry," he said, hoarsely.

Leira pulled in energy through her feet, letting it flow up her spine. Her eyes began to glow as the symbols appeared along her arms, flipping over and over. *Remove the poison on every plane.* She took Matt's hand and held on tight, letting the magic pull her away. She found herself floating in a sea of undulating colors. One of Turner's first lessons kept her relaxed, letting it unfold. *Let the magic do what it has to do. Get out of the way. Trust.*

Her energy wove in and out of the waves of color till it found a pattern that didn't fit the rest, operating on a different frequency. Leira's bright light surrounded it, growing brighter, burning till Leira could feel a warmth in the scar on her belly. She made herself keep breathing steadily, watching the light without concern as it changed to a neon blue before fading altogether.

Whomp!

The energy pulled her back, taking Leira out of the soothing ocean of color and back inside her hallway. She shook her head as her ears popped, a vibration rolling down her spine and out her feet. "That was a trip." Leira swallowed giving herself a second. Correk put his hands on either side of her face, wrapping his energy around her body. "You seem fine."

Leira let go of Matt's hand. "I am fine. I feel like I took a vacation where there was nothing left to worry about."

"It's gone! Look, it's gone." Matt held up his hand and the shiny patch was gone. The dark hair was receding back into his skin. "It worked."

Leira tilted her head to the side. "We helped you, but that's not a good long-term solution. Wolfstan may not know how to pull this trick off on a large scale, but I'll bet he's trying to figure it out. We need a better fix."

There was a scratching at the kitchen door, almost too

faint to hear. "Now what?" Leira went closer as the scratching picked up again. She opened the door and looked down at a large city rat standing on its hind legs holding up a note. "Son of a bitch!" Leira clapped her hands together and reached down, gingerly taking the note from the rat. "I'm sorry, I can't tell if you're the same rat or a different rat but thank you." She looked closer at the rat as his whiskers twitched. "Damn, I still can't tell if you can understand me, but you'd have to, right? No? Nothing."

Leira stood and read the note as the rat waited. *The ring has been safely transferred to the mermaids of the Atlantic Ocean. Distant cousins report Sirius is setting a trap at the dark bar in DC. We're safe and sound and enjoying Miami.*

"Well, fuck me," said Leira, with a crooked smile.

"What does it say?" Correk came closer but the rat squealed, and he backed up again.

"It says that a cockroach has been spotted and a rat knows a mermaid. All is well." Leira smiled, her shoulders relaxing. "We may be able to hurt Wolfstan even more." She bent over, addressing the rat. "Thank you. Do I give you a tip? Anyone have anything shiny?"

"I have a quarter." Matt dug in his pocket and tossed Leira the coin. She offered it to the rat who took it in his paws and bit the edge of it, squealing with delight and running off. "You don't see that every day," said Matt.

"Lately, I see something new every day. I have a text to send to Lois and then let's go back to the party," said Leira. "I think we get to celebrate a couple of victories tonight. Did somebody say something about a boilermaker?"

CHAPTER TWENTY-EIGHT

Lucius towered over the others standing around him. He was in his old leather battle gear, glowering. Surrounding him in a wide circle were a hundred men and women who were all gathered on an old estate belonging to Turner Underwood. It was tucked in Graves Mill, Virginia abutting Shenandoah National Forest.

"Almost everyone looks like they're late for their kid's soccer game, except for the big guy." Leira scooped Yumfuck and put him down on the ground. He took off for the woods, leaving tiny orange footprints.

Correk rolled his eyes and threw up his hands. "Now he's just mocking me. Is there dust in your pocket?"

"Always. Every pocket. Since the day I met you two."

Leira and Correk were standing under a tree with Turner, watching the human shifters keep a wide berth around the large Light Elf. "Why does Lucius have on full battle gear?" Leira shaded her eyes with her hand, shaking her head. "Tell me he's bought some jeans by now. Surely

Big and Tall can fit him. Is this an alpha shifter thing or just a male thing?"

Turner snorted, tapping his cane on a tree root. He was dressed in charcoal grey slacks and a forest green cardigan topped by a matching Fedora. "So many delicious questions. This will be a grand place for a community center," he said, not answering any of them.

Leira bit her lip, sizing up the group. "A community center for shifters. How do you see this working? I bet they chew through everything in less than a month."

Correk let out a guffaw, giving Leira a high five as Turner rolled his eyes, even though he was smiling.

"I admit it's different," said Turner. "That's why it's necessary. They've been vulnerable because they have no central organization. No means to communicate beyond the centuries old method of howling at the moon."

Leira balanced on a tree root, rocking back and forth. "It's hard to believe one of those moms didn't think of a phone tree by now."

"You'd be surprised what shame can stop you from doing." Turner tapped his cane again, pursing his lips. "Shifters have been the sideshow of the magical world long enough. Even they have bought into the storyline that they're not quite magical, not quite human." He pointed his cane at a few of the humans clustered near the outside of the group. "And the ones who were made into shifters by the dark families…"

"Like Matt. He seems to be adjusting well." Correk crossed his arms over his chest.

"He's an exception. Most haven't adapted as well. They have no role models to talk to. No place to hear stories of the great things shifters have done. Did you know that shifters helped turn the tide against Rhazdon seven hundred years ago? It's true."

"I didn't even know that. I've never seen them in any of the paintings in the Light Elves castle."

"That's because they were left out. Queen Saria's doing. There's still a ways to go to get the magical world to catch up to a more open minded way of thinking. This is a start."

Leira winced, watching Lucius growl at a middle aged man who cowered, backing away. "Fuck, even I thought Lucius was gonna bite him."

Turner waved his cane over his head, popping up in front of the shifters.

Leira shook her head and started walking. "They weren't even that far away. Making us look bad, hanging back here."

Correk laughed and put his arm around her shoulders as they trudged over. "I think we're here more as a calming influence today. Let's just enjoy the scenery and make sure Lucius doesn't draw any blood. After they leave, I have a blanket and a bottle of wine in the car."

"So that's why you wanted to drive here. Okay, this is all looking up."

Turner waved his cane, his voice magically amplified, streaming out to the crowd and settling them down. "Thank you all for coming. Lucius, this was more of a casual Friday thing. We've talked about this. There will probably never be an occasion to wear seven hundred year old armor on this world. No worries, but next time..." Turner smiled broadly holding out an arm. "Welcome to the modern age. Seems rather ridiculous, doesn't it? A lot of you work in tech. You know how to write code or create web sites. And yet, in this part of your life it's all just fur and fangs."

Several people looked at the ground, earning a scowl from Turner. "But that ends today. We are going to build a community center here. It's the perfect spot. A place to develop a network, even make a map of where there are other shifters."

"Create an app," said a woman in the back of the crowd.

"Yes! One of those. Those of you who have been shifters for a long time can teach the younger ones."

"We already do that."

"You already teach the wolf side. It's about time, you teach the human... or Light Elf side. Socialize, share stories, information. Become links in a chain. Then no one will ever be able to use you again for their own purposes."

Lucius growled, clenching his hands into fists. Turner gave him a hard shake of his head and he crossed his arms over his chest instead.

"You can even mobilize to do some good. Be proud of who you are. The gates to Oriceran are gradually opening. Someday this world will know about magic and will learn about all of you. Let there be a system already in place. Let there be legends of the great things shifters have done. All of that starts today, right here, with all of you."

Leira laid her head on Correk's shoulder, smiling. "They're creating a family of sorts. I get it."

Turner pulled a long, circular container from inside his sweater. "I have the plans for the new building if anyone wants to see them."

Leira's brows came together, looking at the left and

then the right of Turner's body. "How did he do that? What else does he have in there? Are some clowns actually magical? He's right. I am full of questions."

"I still have a lot to learn as the Fixer," said Correk. "Turner is a legend."

"Give it time."

"We'll need to create committees," said a stocky man in the middle of the crowd.

"And so it begins," said Leira. "Look at Lucius. He actually seems lost. Want to take bets on what committee he ends up on?"

"I'd say hospitality."

Turner looked back at them. "Can it you two."

"Onboarding," whispered Leira, watching the same man direct people to stand in different sections. "Look at them all starting to break into groups. They're gonna be fine. Their inner corporate is coming out. Even stronger than wolf blood. I wonder what a retreat would look like."

Turner let out a huff and turned around to face them, the plans tucked under his arm. "It's clear you two would rather be canoodling somewhere else. Don't bother denying it. I've heard stories from several mermaids."

Leira smiled even as her face reddened.

"Go! Go be happy somewhere else. I think we've passed the danger points." Turner smiled, the wrinkles around his eyes deepening. "Despite everything, this is a very good day. Remember that, both of you. There will be horrors in the world that you won't be able to solve without some anguish. But it doesn't mean you can't find moments of joy."

"Oooh Turner, you better go help." Leira pointed at the

crowd. "Someone is trying to direct Lucius. He looks like a dazed rhino ready to charge."

Turner tsked and strode over to Lucius, talking to him in a soothing voice.

"I think this is our chance to exit," said Correk.

"What about our wine?"

"It'll work just as well back at home. I think they're going to be a while."

"Race you to the car. That won't kick in anyone's prey instinct, will it?"

"Let's find out."

CHAPTER TWENTY-NINE

Leira and Correk dashed past all the large rooms of Turner Underwood's mansion to the door at the end of the hall. They had dropped everything when they got the text. After all this time, today was the day.

They went inside, entering the hidden hallway as Correk began to jog, sweat forming on his lip.

"Okay, usually I'm the one running ahead." Leira kept up with him, hurrying to get to the last door in this hallway. They entered, coming out onto the street from a hundred years ago, and rushed past magicals who stared at their jeans and sneakers. "Oh, come on, you all come from the world out there too." She looked up at Correk's tense face. "Right, not the point today." She took a quick glance around, hoping to see Winland but there were no familiar faces.

Correk took the steps two at a time, pounding on the door and trying the handle. The door flew open on its own and he rushed inside. Leira was right behind him as the door closed and locked itself.

Correk looked in every room, running to the next one. "I'm in here." Turner Underwood's voice echoed from upstairs and Correk took off again, getting to the top as fast as he could. Leira easily kept up, trailing him up the narrow staircase.

"Down the hall on the right," called Turner.

Correk got to the door and stopped cold as Leira collided with his back. "What is it?" She squeezed by him to find Turner Underwood standing over Peyton's prone body. The large Light Elf was lying on an examining table. Turner's hand was firmly on his shoulder, keeping him mildly sedated. A cane with a silver top in the shape of a fairy was leaning against a chair. Harkin was busy adjusting a curved metal hood that was attached to the machinery he had been working on for a very long time.

"We got here as fast as we could," said Correk, breathing hard, his heart pounding.

"You haven't missed anything. We're just about to try it." Turner's expression gave away nothing as he spoke softly to Peyton. "Just a little longer."

Harkin turned and looked at Correk attempting a smile. "It's ready. Where's Lily Sharpton? I wanted her to see this too. She made it possible."

"Lois has her under wraps. It's okay, we'll tell her all about it," said Leira. "Every detail."

"You're the one who never gave up, Dad. Go on, let's do this."

Turner Underwood looked from father to son. "I picked the right Fixer."

"You picked Jackson first." Correk shrugged.

Leira rolled her eyes. "Let's light this rocket."

"I'll have to let go of Peyton," said Turner, "and when I do, he will quickly spiral. There won't be much time."

"What can we do to help?" Leira rubbed her hands together.

"Help me get this hood over the top half of Peyton's body. We need to make sure his head is completely covered by the dome. Careful with it."

Leira and Correk took small measured steps, slowly putting the metal frame down over Peyton's body as Turner moved down, placing his hand on Peyton's leg.

"Give me a minute." Harkin walked back and forth between the machinery and the hood, checking and then rechecking.

"There's no wires. Is it magic?" asked Leira. She recognized the bowl taken from the Dwarf. It was worked into the machinery.

"Blue tooth," Harkin muttered, checking again.

"Harkin, it's now or never." Turner waggled his eyebrows. "Are you willing to take the chance?"

Correk gave his father an encouraging nod as Leira stood by his side, her hands on her hips.

Harkin nodded. "On a count of three. One, two, three…"

Turner lifted his hand and Harkin started the machinery, the artifact's magic winding through the gears and feeding information to the hood. Peyton began to stir, letting out small yelps as the hood began to glow a luminescent green.

Leira's eyes widened as she held her breath, her hand on Correk's shoulder.

But the yelps were quickly replaced with choking

sounds. Peyton struggled inside the hood, his legs beginning to shake. Leira looked at Harkin for guidance and saw the panic in his eyes as he stared at the technology in front of him.

Help him.

Magic instantly raced through her, lighting up her arms and in one swift motion she grabbed Peyton's ankle, creating a bond.

"Leira, no!" Correk reached out to stop her but Turner was even faster. He grabbed his cane, holding it in Correk's way.

Leira felt her Jasper light wrapping around the strains of Peyton's magic, joined by the green trail from Harkin's invention. The three strands wove together, searching out abnormal bursts of light that were blocking the hollow spaces where magic normally flowed freely. Leira could feel the throbbing pain, sharing the experience with Peyton and she clenched her teeth, bearing it with him.

Her back arched, the energy building as Correk pushed at the old Fixer's cane. But Turner was stronger than he looked and held him back. "Let her finish. She can do this. Didn't you sense it, Fixer? Leira commanded her energy without a thought. That's the first time she's done that. She's made a leap into a new connection with her power."

On and on, the woven strands sought out the fractured light, healing the spaces till they came to the last string.

Peyton began to settle down, his body relaxing. Leira let go, her chest heaving up and down from the exertion as the symbols settled down. She rushed to one side of the hood trying to lift it. Turner lowered his cane and Correk went to the other side, helping her, setting the device on the floor.

"Careful with that," said Harkin, but he was already maneuvering around it. His focus was on Peyton, who lay motionless on the table. Harkin approached him cautiously, slowly putting two fingers against his neck. A look of relief washed over him. "Normal. For the first time in a hundred years. Just normal." He put his rough hands against Peyton's face. "Peyton. Peyton, are you in there?"

Leira took Correk's hand, lacing her fingers in his, waiting for something. Anything.

Peyton's eyes blinked open and he looked directly at Harkin, holding his gaze. "You did it," he whispered. His voice was hoarse, but the words were clear.

"Well I'll be…" Turner's voice broke, and he waved his hand in front of his face as he shook his head. "Two moons."

Harkin searched his friend's face as he choked out the words. "I'm sorry. I was wrong."

Peyton put his hand over Harkin's and tried to lift his head, grimacing in pain. "You saved my life. I knew you would never give up."

Leira pressed a hand to her chest. "You knew what was going on all this time."

"I only understood bits and pieces." Harkin helped Peyton sit up as the Light Elf groaned from the effort. "Every muscle aches."

"You had a lot of energy running through you." Leira slid her hand down to the scar on her belly. "That much voltage can be a bitch."

He squeezed his eyes shut, pressing a hand to his back. Inch long bolts of green and blue lightning sparked around his head. He ducked each time it happened, patting his hair.

"That's normal, Peyton." Harkin slid pillows behind his back. "Your magic is still recalibrating. It'll take a while and to be honest I can't be sure what kind of magic you'll have when the process is complete. We'll have to find out."

"It's still hard to think straight."

"That should pass in a day or two. I'll stay here till it does."

Turner's face lit up and he smacked his lips, nodding with delight. "I have an idea. Harkin, your efforts may help us defeat Wolfstan Humphrey in the end." Turner picked up his hat from a table and placed it on his head.

"Going somewhere?" Leira wrinkled her brow. "Tell us the idea, at least."

"That's not the way he works," said Correk. "You know that."

"I'll send someone to stay with Peyton. He won't be alone." Turner gave a pat to the top of his hat. "There's somewhere else I need to be." He left the room, swinging his cane.

Leira went to stop him but the hallway was empty. "Another time." She came back in and stood next to Correk. "I wanted to tell him about Sirius and the rat."

"It's Turner Underwood. The rat probably stopped at his house first. Let's just be here for a little while."

Correk watched Peyton struggle to find the right words, a relief washing over him. "You have a blank slate, Harkin. You can decide who you want to be next."

"Helping Peyton and getting back to you were all I wanted for a very long time. I don't even know what was third on the list."

"Well then, let's make a new list. We can do it together. Like a family."

CHAPTER THIRTY

Sirius waited in the shadows, his long dark coat buttoned tight against the sudden drop in temperature. The nights were growing colder. A trap had been set for a few of the younger magical cousins in the dark families. He still had a debt to pay to Wolfstan, and so far, nothing had been delivered. Time was running short.

Laughter came from the other end of the alley, floating on the breeze. A witch and two wizards were taking a shortcut to a bar haunted by young dark magicals. It was in the basement of a townhouse in Georgetown protected by wards that didn't let out any sound and alerted the management if Silver Griffins were approaching. The metal door would melt into place, vanishing until there was an all-clear.

Sirius moved along the wall, waiting for his moment. His entire focus was on his prey or he would have noticed the handle on the bar's door begin to flatten out. He ran his hand over his silver hair, neatly slicked back against his skull and licked his dry lips. "Now or never," he said, with a shrug, stepping out into the center of the alley. He raised his wand, ready to send out a pulse of energy powerful enough to knock them back. Sirius shook his head. "Need them alive. More trouble, but if that's the deal," he muttered.

The wave of energy undulated rapidly down the alley, knocking against the young magicals. It pushed in on their chests making it hard to breathe. A signature move for Sirius. He kept his wand level, concentrating as he walked closer, waiting for the trio to finally pass out. "Finally!" he shouted. "Some fucking thing is breaking in my direction."

He slipped past the entrance to the bar, the door completely gone, blending with the metal frame around it. The young witch reached her hand toward Sirius, her eyes pleading but that only made Sirius laugh. "Why is that always a last move?"

"Seen enough?" Lois stepped out of the shadows from the other end of the alley.

Sirius startled, his smile quickly changing to his more customary scowl. "Not now! Why does my damn sister always have to spoil things?" he shouted, gripping his wand tighter. He was still unwilling to release his quarry. The younger of the wizards finally lay down his head, his lips turning blue.

The sound of high heels on old pavers clicked and clacked behind Sirius at the opposite end of the alley. His stomach soured as he recognized the footfalls. He lowered his wand, releasing the spell as the witch gasped for air, crawling toward the unconscious wizard. The third magical lay on his back, stunned, taking in sips of air, his eyes wide.

"Hello, Ariana." Sirius didn't bother to turn around as he let out an exasperated sigh.

"Cousin. I told the Silver Griffins they were liars. Normally, that's true. But it appears this time they got it right. You're hunting your own kind. That's going to be a problem for me."

Sirius glanced over his shoulder, keeping an eye on Lois. "Looks like you two ladies came alone. I've escaped worse. I might even have the pleasure of taking one of you down and salvaging this evening."

"I doubt that." Ariana struck the palm of her hand with her wand, over and over again. "But you were our fearless leader for a long time. I'll concede you know a few tricks. Well, I know a few as well. One of them is, don't bring a knife to a gun fight."

"You're quoting old movies to me now," roared Sirius, whipping his wand in a circle, spraying the alley with bouncing fireballs in every direction. Lois easily dodged them, the yellow and orange lights briefly illuminating the dark alley. Sirius pivoted to where he could see both witches approaching him, his wand out, ready to strike.

Ariana smiled, not moving from where she stood. Sirius narrowed his gaze, confused.

"I learned to ask for help, Cousin," said Ariana, tilting her head. "I brought the big, furry, hungry guns." She smiled, raising her arm. Pairs of yellow eyes appeared in the dark behind her, crowding the alley. Sirius felt a cold chill go down his spine and he turned to run, but there were more shifters running on padded paws to take their place behind Lois.

"Another day, then," said Sirius, starting to open a

portal. But when he waved his wand, the light fizzled, going nowhere. "What the fuck? Who is powerful enough to do that?"

"Sic him," shouted Ariana, flicking her painted red nail in Sirius' direction. A roar erupted from both sides of the alley as the shifters flowed around the two witches, closing in on their target. Sirius' eyes grew wide with horror and he swung his wand, pushing back the first layer of wolves, but there were five more to replace them, coming from both sides.

"No, not like this." Sirius gritted his teeth and kept fighting. But the wolves were on him in no time, tearing at his expensive black coat, clawing at his flesh, disturbing his neatly combed hair.

Lois hesitated for a moment, but she finally lifted the whistle in her hand and blew. Only the shifters heard the call and they obeyed it, stopping their frenzy. They waited, still baring their fangs that were now dipped in blood.

Lois walked slowly over to the wounded Sirius, the wolves making a path for her. She stood over him, stepping on his injured arm, cut to ribbons and waited for him to cry out in pain. "That was for Lacey Trader. Death is too easy a solution for you, Sirius."

"He's all yours now." Ariana made her way closer to her fallen cousin.

"Trevilsom awaits you. You will never get out, brother. May you live for a thousand more years staring at those cold walls." Lois opened a portal to the island outside Trevilsom's gates. On the other side, two guards wearing hoods stepped through and lifted Sirius' body as he groaned in pain.

They dragged him back through the portal as Lois followed them. She stopped, holding open the sides. "Ariana, you and I are related, and we have more in common than you think. Wolfstan has targeted both of us. Learn from it."

The portal closed, sending sparks skittering across the alley as the entrance to the bar reshaped itself. A young wizard came out of the door lighting a cigarette as the pack of shifters turned their heads in unison to look at him.

The wizard let the cigarette fall out of his mouth as he slowly backed down the stairs and went back inside.

Ariana laughed, petting one of the large furry heads. "This is going to be a very long friendship."

Turner Underwood watched from the shadows, a feeling of dread coming over him. "Ariana, you may prove to be the more difficult enemy. For another day." He twirled his cane, and in a moment, he was gone.

Get sneak peeks, exclusive giveaways, behind the scenes content, and more. PLUS you'll be notified of special **one day only fan pricing** on new releases.

Sign up today to get free stories.

Visit: https://marthacarr.com/read-free-stories/

It's September 11th, a day of remembrance, in the strangest of years. Nineteen years ago, 2,977 people died in a matter of hours from a senseless terrorist attack meant to make us afraid. It took our breath away but instead of instilling fear, it sent a wave of unity across the country. We came together as a nation almost seamlessly, overnight. We grieved as a nation of millions.

There's a photograph of a row of townhouses on September 11th, and then on the day after the same homes have American flags flying from every front porch. We remembered our common bonds and it meant something.

In this strange year, 196,134 people have died from the novel coronavirus, so far. There's a chance this winter may bring more grim news. But instead of bringing us together, somehow the details have pulled us all apart. We seem to have forgotten what makes us similar and instead we are endlessly staring at, shouting about what makes us different.

That's ironic.

What makes us different is also what makes the United States unique. A country almost completely made up of immigrants. Some from two hundred years ago, and others from last week and every time in between. Most of us have come from somewhere else, carrying our heritage and our customs with us. Over the generations we have shared all of it. We are the only country in the world that has this rarified status. We chose to be together and live as fellows among fellows, instead of a monarchy or a dictatorship. Instead a democracy.

We have argued, we have struggled, we have created wonderous things. And when something has threatened our democracy, the base of what connects all of us, we have fought together to defend it. Differences were no longer a point of contention but a kind of inventory to see how someone could contribute to a common cause.

We can do that again.

Instead of wondering what you might take from me, I can ask myself what I can give to help you. It takes a certain amount of courage and trust in something bigger to be willing to share or sacrifice, particularly in this strangest of years.

I write about magic because I love it, and I have since I was a little kid. But maybe not for the reasons you think. I love the kind of magic that happens when a human being (not an Elf or a Witch), stops thinking about themselves, and instead rushes forward to help another human being. To pull a stranger from a burning car or donate a kidney to someone we heard needed one. Some call that grace. I happen to call it magic. It's so powerful that when the rest of us see it, we are transformed as well.

Then there's the bigger magic that happens when we come together as a group. Ordinary people who decide to do something to help like build a playground or repair a house or offer shelter after a flood. Or in my case, when a woman I never met took my application for a grant I needed for an operation to save my life. The surgeons refused to do anything unless I was approved, and the clock was ticking.

Without a request from me, this young woman chose to walk from desk to desk and building to building waiting for each needed signature to get me approved in a day. Normally approval took six weeks, which would have cost me my life. I was dying from an aggressive cancer at the time. Six weeks would have tipped me over the edge. That woman's grace saved my life. She never asked where I was from or what I was like before she chose to help. I have no idea what her story was or if her life was going well. It wasn't our differences that made her act. It was our common bond.

I believe in my bones that's who we really are and this democracy that we cherish is the best representation of it.

In this strangest of years, may we all remember that spark of humanity we all possess and use it to remember our powerful magic. May we come together to build something wonderous that future generations will marvel at, not only because of what it is, but because of when we chose to do it. In the midst of so much chaos and grief and uncertainty, we took a chance on ourselves and each other. A kind of definition of democracy in America. More adventures to follow.

AUTHOR NOTES - MICHAEL ANDERLE

WRITTEN SEPTEMBER 13, 2020

First, THANK YOU for not only reading our stories but all the way back to our author notes, as well.

The first part of fall finally hit here in Las Vegas this last week, and the night time temps dipped into the 60s and the daytime went up to low 90s.

In short, the weather was a tease.

Temperatures are back up in the 100s, but for two days, it was almost comfortable outside. I am both happy for the change and not sure how to feel about it. On the one hand, I will be able to work outside and enjoy the weather in the backyard again.

But other options like swimming will be severely curtailed. Why, you ask, when the temperatures will still be in the 90s for at least a few weeks?

Because in the dry air here in the desert, I freeze if the tiniest breeze hits my skin. My body acts as if coming out of the pool is a type of torture test. Or perhaps a race.

A race to see how fast I can get enough water off my skin to stop shivering. It's embarrassing. I shudder (no pun intended) when in the future little grandkids are making fun of granddad and how he is such a wuss when it comes to playing in the water.

"How can you write characters that are so badass, only to shiver in cold water?!" they will cry.

I'll have to explain that over the years, the bad guys kept hitting me with their freeze and death rays, that I had to hang up my super-awesome-hero-guardian cape and retire. The effects of all of those fights left me a broken-bodied man.

Huh, maybe being a granddad and lying (u-hum. *Telling stories*) won't be so bad after all.

When you get a chance, hug those in your family, and with thought or deed in your community. It's suggested if you sow good deeds / feelings to others, they germinate, grow, and come back as a harvest.

I wish you the best day, the best week, and the best rest of 2020.

If you need a smile, just imagine the frustrations my kids will have when their children come home after staying with Grandpa and having to explain that no, grandpa didn't really fly to the moon in a special UFO he captured along with two elves named L'eff and L'eff-to.

I never could tell those two apart.

Ad Aeternitatem,
Michael Anderle

For Hire: Teachers for special school in Virginia countryside.

Must be able to handle teenagers with special abilities.

Cannot be afraid to discipline werewolves, wizards, elves and other assorted hormonal teens.

Apply at the School of Necessary Magic.

AVAILABLE ON AMAZON RETAILERS

If smart phones and GPS rule the world - why am I hunting a magic compass to save the planet?

Austin Detective Maggie Parker has seen some weird things in her day, but finding a surly gnome rooting through her garage beats all.

Her world is about to be turned upside down in a frantic search for 4 Elementals.

Each one has an artifact that can keep the Earth humming along, but they need her to unite them first.

Unless the forces against her get there first.

AVAILABLE ON AMAZON AND IN KINDLE UNLIMITED!

Other series in the Oriceran Universe:

SOUL STONE MAGE

THE KACY CHRONICLES

MIDWEST MAGIC CHRONICLES

THE FAIRHAVEN CHRONICLES

I FEAR NO EVIL

THE DANIEL CODEX SERIES

SCHOOL OF NECESSARY MAGIC

SCHOOL OF NECESSARY MAGIC: RAINE CAMPBELL

ALISON BROWNSTONE

FEDERAL AGENTS OF MAGIC

SCIONS OF MAGIC

THE UNBELIEVABLE MR. BROWNSTONE

OTHER BOOKS BY JUDITH BERENS

OTHER BOOKS BY MARTHA CARR

**JOIN THE ORICERAN UNIVERSE FAN GROUP ON
FACEBOOK!**